Psyche

A love story

Gerry Haines

Contents

1. An Explanation   1

2. Meeting Psyche   2

3. Meeting Tony   10

4. The Trouble With Psyche   18

5. Liverpool   27

6. Transition   36

7. Psyche After All   50

8. Lawyers and Exits   67

9. George's Question   76

10. Così   84

11. Nehemiah   90

12. Unfixable Bethan   98

13. Homecomings   113

14. Tony Under the Stars   123

15. Into The Dark   139

16. Bethan By The River   151

17. Settlement   160

18. Expulsion and Flight 177

19. Unsettlement 188

20. After Dido 200

21. Flight 208

22. Resettlement 220

23. "She's Back" 227

24. Connection 234

Thanks and Acknowledgements 237

Playlist 238

Chapter One

An Explanation

This morning, I looked at myself in the mirror. It wasn't just a passing glance, or a vanity check. I watched the face of an old man looking steadily back at me. I haven't got long to live, not necessarily in any clinical sense, simply that I am old. For once, rather than scurrying off to get things done before I do croak, I watched myself thinking about what my life might mean after I'm dead, what my life might have meant to others, what those others mean to me.

Sometimes it is difficult to understand the difference we have made to our world as we pass through it. "Had we the gift to see ourselves as others see us..." It might be the purest egotism to ponder such things, but I doubt many people, other than saints and sages, are immune to it. I want to get the clearest focus I can on the lives of three people I loved, and the only way I can do so is by telling a story. After all, each of us is a collection of stories, told by us and about us.

There's no one else left to tell this story about a cult, a voice, and the patterns of love and despair that bound us three together. I shall attempt to tell their story; I'll try to find their true colours. I'll do it simply; I'm too bloody old to fuss around with post-modernism or any other -ism.

Chapter Two

Meeting Psyche

My friend Tony's father, George, had a large second-floor flat in Kensington, on a quiet street a couple of blocks back from a busy through-road. It was a haven for occasional post-party, post-pub collapses during the school holidays. George was impossibly cool, as people say far too easily nowadays, but he was cool in our terms, back then. He was quite a short, slight figure, with dark hair and a tanned face. I used to wonder if his origins were Italian, or maybe Spanish, given his name. It would have felt impertinent to ask.

Amused, gentle but firm with young idiots, unflappable, he had a way of looking directly at you for a moment before answering a question. I used to think he wouldn't say anything unless he had something to say. But I mustn't make him seem remote or stand-offish. He was very generous, in that unobtrusive way that seems to come more easily to truly confident people, because they don't need you to acknowledge their generosity. He was a very busy and successful man, but on a few occasions he sat down and listened to me, speaking only a little and always to the point. For those conversations I shall always be grateful.

George's living room was the first one I'd seen with two large sofas opposite each other. It was following an evening at The Elephant and a short night sleeping it off on one of those sofas, that Tony woke me with a cup of tea, and I sort of met his sister.

"By the way, oik, you were rather rude to my sister last night," he said, pointing over my shoulder. I turned to look, and said, before I could focus on her, "Really? I do beg your pardon, or is he making it up to embarrass me?"

"Perhaps he means you ignored me." A quiet, low voice. I still couldn't see her properly, so I rolled over, stood up and turned round.

A lot of long dark hair. A pale face, chin down. Large eyes, which looked up and out at mine briefly, and then down at my bare feet.

I lurched into speech. "Yes, that was rude of me, have we met before? If so, it was inexcusable. I'm so sorry. I can't think why I would ignore someone like you," I burbled. I could hear Tony sniggering behind me.

"He means someone who looks like you," he said delightedly, "don't you, Gerry?"

A smile from the girl. "Shut up, Tony." She walked to the window and looked out. Slim, quite tall, graceful. "Why not get the poor man some breakfast. What sort of host are you?"

I ran out of things to say. "Well, I do have to go fairly soon, so maybe…" No answer from the window. "My name's Gerry," I said desperately.

She turned back to me. "I'd gathered that," she said, and swept her hair back from her face. I fought against blushing, which never works, does it? I'd have been quite happy to say nothing and simply look at her but I had to say something.

"And what's your… I mean, might one ask your name?"

I sounded like a pompous Edwardian.

"You might," said Tony, as he came in and put a croissant on the table. He was really enjoying himself. "But she might not tell you because her name embarrasses her. She's called Psyche."

She looked at him for a moment without expression. "Piss off," was all she said, quietly, and Tony tried to laugh it off but it caught him. I knew him too well not to see it. I tried to smooth things over.

"I think it's a lovely name," I said. I could hear myself trying too hard. "And so unusual. Tell me about it?"

"I don't think so, not today. Maybe next time you ignore me," she said, but with a smile. She walked to the door - almost seemed to glide, like her father - and was gone.

I busied myself with breakfast so as not to look at Tony too directly. Eventually I looked up, ready for some fencing.

"Well?" he said, grinning most irritatingly.

"Well what?"

"Whaddyer think?"

"Do you know what a Pander is?"

"Cuddly Chinese bear."

"Ah, of course, you're in the science sixth. "Troilus and Cressida," look it up, oaf. Pander in the sense of pimp, for your own sister now?"

"You should be so lucky."

"Yes, shouldn't I, and now we know where all the looks in your family landed up, you insolent gargoyle."

And so on. Eventually I thanked him for putting me up, threw a sofa cushion at him and went back to the suburbs with an aching head. What did I think? I didn't know. As the Tube rattled south, I thought maybe something significant might have just happened to me at last, then I thought I was making something out of nothing.

Then the analysis abruptly stopped, and a simple truth erupted. She was very beautiful and, like her father, very cool.

"Johnny" Walker wasn't really named Johnny, but who can resist the alias of a whisky when you're 18? Johnny said he thought Psyche was good enough looking but nothing special. I could see he was trying to play man of the world. I ignored him. One of the others, I forget who, said he thought she was "a bit of all right," and did I think I stood a chance?

I thought probably not, but didn't say so. She seemed to be part of a Floating World beyond my reach, drifting through that big, airy flat. A real classy bird, as Johnny Walker would have admitted, had he not been playing Mr Experienced. And I certainly wanted to see her again. I tried to use reason. I told myself: you've seen her for about five embarrassing minutes. You looked a wreck, having slept in your clothes. You tried much too hard, and she went off to her room.

Her room! Visions of that shiny black hair lying across pure white bed-linen. A couple of days later, I rang Tony from a noisy pub.

"What do you want, scruff bag?"

"I'm prepared to buy you a pint, if you get over here."

"What? Is it Christmas? Where are you?"

"The Elephant, where do you think?"

"I'm there in five and it's a pint of best, not that horrible cooking bitter."

A pleasant enough hour ensued, after which we decided to drive to Heathrow, or "LAP" as we would-be sophisticates called it, for a coffee.

"The cafés around here are just too crowded, man, let's go."

So we did, man, in Tony's little car. A pointless expedition, you might think; but there were five of us, including two girls. One of whom was Psyche.

At the airport, I sidled off for a pee and Tony moved into the next bin. "Have you managed to find it, boy?" I said. It was an old routine.

"I'm sure it's in here somewhere, give me a minute. But can I be serious for a moment?"

"I'm all ears."

"Do you like my sister?"

My heart started pounding. I paused a moment, thinking of a cool or well-balanced answer. Keep it simple.

"Yes, I sure do."

"Well, despite your lamentable debut performance, I think you might stand a chance. Give her a bell next week and ask her to the flicks."

"You know, you're not such a twat after all. Thanks. I'll do the same for you some day."

Though I knew I couldn't, wouldn't, and wouldn't need to.

From my diary of those days: *So when we drove back from the airport, I sat next to her in the front. It was marvellous to sit with a girl again, watching the lights and the road flash by. She leaned her head on my shoulder, dark hair falling forward and I breathed in the scent of her scalp, along with a light perfume. I confess I am very taken with her.*

I also confess now, which I was too coy to do in the diary back then, that I had a very firm erection before we'd cleared Hounslow and I was terrified she'd notice it. I don't think she did, or was too polite, or quietly amused, to mention it. Tony dropped me off outside my home, which was helpful of him. It meant I could shuffle off with my trophy hard-on unnoticed. I gave her cheek a little peck through the car window and she patted my hand gently. I drifted through the next day or two. It had started well, I told myself. I wasn't sure what "it" was, but I was hopeful, elated and nervous.

Two evenings later, a Thursday, my next evening off from bar work, I was round at George's again. It was a short visit. Psyche had rehearsed all day in a choir and was due to do so all the next day. We sat and talked and tried to ignore Tony, which was never easy, as he would happily admit. She was tired, but we deepened our acquaintance. I tried the self-deprecating mode, hoping she would say to her friends "and he's so modest, too."

After we'd talked about books, music and dance, she said "but in fact, you're very clever, aren't you?"

I blushed as never before. "Well, I..."

"Are you going to Oxford or Cambridge, then? Tony said you'd applied."

"Er, no. They turned their backs on me, the blind fools."

"Oh. What did they say?"

"They pointed out you need Latin to read English at Oxbridge and my amateur clown of a headmaster hadn't noticed."

"Nevertheless, you are clever, aren't you?" Teasingly: "Come on. Admit it."

A level look from dark eyes. "We'll see," I answered lamely. "Clever enough for Liverpool University, I hope."

We chatted on about interests, all the things you're supposed to discuss to keep your eyes off her breasts, her legs...but that's not entirely fair to my teen self. She did enchant me, as in: she put a spell on me. She had an absorbing, quiet intensity I had never encountered before. And when she listened, it was almost fierce.

Eventually, I said "So what's the difficulty with your name? I know I had a bit of a splutter about it when we met, but I really do think it's a lovely name, and very unusual."

She looked sharply at me for a moment.

"Do you actually know who Psyche was?"

Thank goodness, I did. "Well yes, as it happens. A mortal woman, so beautiful even Aphrodite was jealous of her. Wife of Eros. Persephone double-crossed her. She died, but Eros saved her and took her to

Olympus. She became goddess of the soul. Psyche was more beautiful than Helen of Troy, even."

"And you wonder why the name embarrasses me?"

A sudden moment of unexpected boldness arrived in me, I didn't know from where. I reached over the coffee table, took her hand and looked into that lovely pale face. I paused.

"But Psyche you are ... the loveliest girl I have ever seen. Anywhere. Certainly more beautiful than crummy old Aphrodite."

Now it was her turn to blush. As the pink spread up her usual pallor, she looked down.

"Should I thank you?"

"Don't you dare. What, for speaking the truth?"

We sat there quietly for a few moments. Mercifully, Tony was getting a drink. Her blush subsided. "I've not blushed like that for a long time."

"Oh, I blush all the time, I'm hopeless."

She smiled. "You are not hopeless. But what do you think the girls at school called me?"

I just gazed at her.

"Psycho."

"Were you at a boarding school?"

"Yes."

"Thought so. I expect you were pretty good at ignoring them."

"Eventually."

"And at music college, now?"

"Oh, we are all painfully adult, respectable and polite," she said, with a trace of a smile that suggested otherwise. "And we work very hard."

"I'd love to hear you sing."

She looked pleased. "We'll see," was all she said.

I'm pleased I was sensitive enough to clear off in good time so she could sleep; lovely voices need looking after.

Chapter Three

Meeting Tony

The origins of my close relationship with Tony go back to boarding school, but don't be misled. This isn't a tale of midnight dorm feasts and crushes on Matron, and our school, Dallinghoo, was seriously short of any kind of wizardry. Neither was it a nest of future prime ministers. Moreover, the impact of being a boarder, aged nine, was something I only really began to understand later in life.

I remember lying in bed while my mother showed me the new things she had bought for school. There was my name, Gerald Haines, in little red letters on strips of white cloth tape, sewn into the collars of strange grey and white shirts. No one called me Gerald, or used my surname. I was bemused because I didn't understand much about what was going to happen.

I didn't understand much more when my parents took me to Liverpool Street station and handed me over to a woman called Matron. Funny name, I remember thinking. I sat in the railway compartment with some of the junior school party, not saying much at all. Boys were chattering round me; they stopped to ask who I was, or where I lived. One boy told me "Cheer up. You'll be okay." But I felt numbed rather than sad. My new shirt made my neck itch. My shoulders seemed suddenly and oddly visible to me and awkward, as if they weren't really mine. I felt uncomfortably aware of my self.

Everything at the school was new and painfully strange. The house where I slept smelled of new paint and disinfectant. I was told to change my shoes for slippers and shown the way upstairs. I saw the top blanket from my bed at home on a strange bed in a large room full of several other beds.

"This is your dorm, Haines," said Matron, as she attempted to settle me in with her kindly, bustly manner, "and this little locker is just yours, for all your own things."

Haines. Is that who I was now?

I remember moving more slowly than usual, watching, listening, anxious to learn the new routines and rituals. I remember a kindly word here and there. Being new was intensely tiring and I slept really well the first few nights. I don't remember feeling anything other than bemused and numbed, until the first weekly session in which we were told to write home. I managed "Dear Mummy and Daddy" and then big wet blotches and ink runs began to appear on the page in front of me. It took me a moment to realise they came from my own tears.

I knew better than to howl or make a fuss. Eventually, a hand fell on my shoulder and a fresh sheet of paper appeared in front of me. "When you're ready, old chap, give it another try, eh?" I sat there with tears running down my nose. I tried not to gulp and gasp and I did manage to write a very short letter. But the damage was done. From then on, boys saw me as a cry-baby.

It wasn't, by the standards of the mid-1950s, a particularly brutal school and masters did intervene if they were on the scene, but small boys in a herd can easily turn on an outsider. As individuals, they could just as quickly and easily be friendly again. I learned a lot, instinctively and quickly, about aspects of basic human psychology. I got used to the rhythm of school term and home holidays and I wasn't miserable all the time. But I remember dreaming I was back at school when I was at home, and waking up with a feeling of mild dread, a sort of heavy unwillingness.

Two things helped me. I discovered that I could play cricket. In any school, and perhaps most of all in a boarding school, you need an identity: Strong man/bully, musician, class clown, brain-box, eccentric...something. I began to emerge as a sportsman.

And then I met Tony Palmera. Tony was my age, but he didn't join until he was 12, a year before the move to the senior school. I took to him almost at once. We were in the same class and I liked his quiet sense of self-possession. He didn't flare up, as I did all too often, and he was easy to talk to. And it didn't pay to cross him. He was determined, rather than noticeably tough looking.

One day I'd got into a shouting match with a couple of my tormentors and one of them, Jenks, had me shoved up against the cricket pavilion wall. He was starting to shake me hard by the shoulders so my head banged against the wall, when a voice came from behind him.

"Leave him alone."

"Fuck off and mind your own business."

"I said, leave him alone."

Jenks turned around and grabbed Tony's lapels. He started to say, "Do you want some – " when Tony broke the boy's hold and pushed him hard backwards against the wall. Jenks' friend, Coulter, swung wildly at Tony, missed, and Tony punched him in the face. Coulter sat down abruptly with blood starting to run from his nose.

"I'll get you for that!" Jenks charged at Tony, who sidestepped, tripped him up and punched him on the side of his head when he tried to get up again. He sat back on the ground, looking woozy.

"Will you?" said Tony. He was in a state of cold and frightening anger. "I don't think so."

He massaged his hand and looked down at the two boys.

"You can start some stupid vendetta if you like, or you can drop it. Leave us alone, or I'll hit you hard next time."

By this time, Coulter was starting to cry and his nose was bleeding down his shirt.

As we walked off, I tried to thank him. "People like that need to learn the hard way, Gerry." He'd never used my first name before. "Else they'll be cruel bullies for life."

Jenks and Coulter sneaked, of course, and tried to pretend Tony had picked on them, but they had form. Tony got some pious jaw about the peaceful resolution of arguments. He thought that sounded a bit thick, coming thirteen years after the end of the war in which the master concerned had, we knew, been decorated for bravery.

"Did he peacefully resolve his arguments with any Messerchmitts?" muttered Tony when he told me about it. Adolescents often have a powerful sense of natural justice and he was irritated to be told off rather than congratulated, for dealing with two notorious little thugs.

And that was the thing about Tony. He always seemed to know where he was going and how to get there, even when he didn't. Sometimes this determination got him into big trouble.

A year or two later, we were sitting in our classroom early one evening doing "prep," or homework you'd call it if you were at home. Tony had been writing to a girl back home. He'd be the last boy to boast about it, but he was very pleased with progress. The letters between them were pretty warm.

We had a very clever but capricious young classics master, Dan Jervis, not long down from Oxford. How he landed up at Dallinghoo instead of a school much further up the ladder, we couldn't find out.

But we liked him. Or we used to. Jervis was on duty that evening, stalking up and down between the rows of desks, bored out of his head I expect. He looked over Tony's shoulder.

"You're not supposed to be writing letters, Palmera."

"Sorry sir. I'll put it away. I'd finished my prep, and I just thought – "

Jervis snatched the letter up from the desk, and began looking it over.

"May I have that back please, sir, it's private, and – "

"I'm not surprised it's private. Listen to this, boys..."

I was very tense by now. I could see Tony wasn't going to put up with it. He was white with anger.

Jervis got three words into it before Tony leapt up and snatched the letter back. Jervis swung his hand back and slapped Tony hard across the face. Tony swung a fist back at him, but fortunately, he missed. Jervis grabbed his wrist, and hauled him out of the room.

I snatched up the letter from where Tony had dropped it, folded it and put it in my pocket. The room was very quiet.

"Will he get expelled?"

"That was really unfair."

"Read us a bit, Gerry, go on."

"No."

"Oh, come on, just – "

"Fuck off. It's private."

Nods of agreement.

Meanwhile Tony had been taken to his housemaster. He was told he was lucky not to be expelled. He was then beaten so hard blood ran down his leg. Tony showed us the scabs on his bum. He didn't bother to comment on it or rail against Jervis or his housemaster. But a day or two later, Jervis came up to Tony. Tony watched him approach and smiled. Jervis smiled back.

"No hard feelings, Palmera, eh? Next time, let's keep the boxing to the ring, shall we?" He held out his hand. He was trying to be "a sport."

A couple of boys were walking past and saw what happened next. Which was nothing. Tony knew he'd won. He carried on smiling.

"Good afternoon sir," he said. He turned away and walked off.

Jervis never forgave Tony and tried to provoke him a couple of times. Tony stepped round him, changed the subject, or said nothing.

His housemaster tried to take it further. According to Tony, it went like this:

"Palmera! Come here. I understand you snubbed Mr Jervis."

"No sir, I wished him good afternoon."

"You wouldn't shake his hand."

"I'm sorry sir, I didn't realise it was compulsory."

"If you cheek me, boy, I will beat you again, just as hard as before."

"In that case, you need to know that I sent my father a photo of the scabs and scars on my bottom. He is consulting a lawyer. If you'll pardon me, sir, without telling you your own business, it doesn't pay to cross my father."

"Can't take it, eh, Palmera? Have to whine to Daddy?"

"So it seems, sir. It's time for chapel, isn't it? I wouldn't want to make us late. Good evening, sir," and he walked out.

Tony sustained this chilly insolent politeness for the rest of the term.

At this point, I'd never met Tony's father. A couple of weeks later, a large black car glided up to the school. A slight figure got out and walked into Tony's house. He asked for the housemaster. "He is expecting me," he said quietly. While he was in the housemaster's study, several boys tried to hear what was being said. The housemaster, whose nickname was Satan, was heard to raise his voice a couple of times. The eavesdroppers couldn't hear a word of what George said.

The following week, Tony was moved from Satan's boarding house to mine, which pleased me but clearly didn't please Satan, who tried glowering at Tony, seeking to wrong-foot him, trying to get him to be cheeky.

"Perhaps it amuses the old bastard," Tony commented to me. "He's getting nowhere."

Tony's admirable characteristics were plain, to me. He was surprisingly tough, kept his cool and he was clever - certainly cleverer than the two masters who had assaulted him. He also had an interestingly wealthy father.

Jervis left the school at the end of the term, with no explanation given. We found out later that it was Tony's father who had paid for an expensive refurbishment of the music room. Some of us thought this was quid pro quo and questioned Tony, who said nothing.

But Tony wasn't universally popular. A lot of the boys thought he was stand-offish, not a joiner-in. He wasn't particularly good at sports; he was good at maths.

From my diary: *The thing about Tony is that we don't always see eye-to-eye. In fact, sometimes we argue quite fiercely about all sorts of things. But it doesn't affect how we feel about each other au fonde. [sic] Our friendship just sails on. I think he's rather impressed by my cricketing skills though he would never admit it. He does wander over to the boundary if we are playing at home and watches me demolish (sometimes!) the bowling. I'm rather impressed by his scientific abilities. They think he'll get into Cambridge. From Dallinghoo! That'd be close to a first. I asked him once how he learned to fight. "Horrible little prep school," was all he said. I am impressed by this ability, I don't have it. It's not to do with conventional boxing stuff or judo or anything.*

It was, I can now see, a matter of speed, along with total concentration and commitment. He once said to me, "If you get into a fight, just win it. If you can't win, don't get into a fight." And of course, sometimes he got hurt – though mostly it was the other bloke who suffered more.

We didn't talk much about families. I used to grumble about my parents to him, until he snapped back at me:

"You're bloody lucky and you don't realise it."

I stopped dead and looked at him. He went a bit red.

"My mother died a few years ago. That's why I'm here, really, and not at the day school I was at before. My father didn't think he could look after me well enough. He travels a lot for his business."

I didn't know what to say. I said I was really sorry.

"Oh, forget it. But that's why I don't go on about families too much. Maybe one day. Not yet."

I could see he was trying not to cry.

"Come on, I'll buy you a Coke and ice-cream."

"You're the last of the big spenders, Gerry."

Tony and I were close friends at school for four or five years and we were accused of being "bum boys," as gay relationships were so charmingly termed. We weren't, and contrary to stereotype, there were, as far as I remember, very few clearly gay boys. The chemistry of close friendships between boys in adolescence is no doubt complex, possibly involving submerged homoerotic elements and so forth. Certainly, the bond between us was powerful.

Chapter Four

The Trouble With Psyche

My diaries from this time were mostly an unbearable read, so I disposed of them. They were boring and embarrassing by turns and if I couldn't bear to read them, who could? Page after page of self-analysis, anxiety, longings and very few interesting details about the life around me. But before I ditched them, before I felt queasy from an overdose of 18-year-old self-centred callowness, I re-read the pages about meeting Psyche.

Here was some genuine pain; a vivid regret at my failure to communicate and a baffling sadness about her that was only understandable to me much later. For once, I was writing about my life as it was lived in the company of others.

A week or so after the Heathrow expedition, I rang George's doorbell. Psyche had agreed to the flicks, as Tony suggested. I felt reasonably confident, more so than usual.

Tony opened the door. He lacked his usual cheeky grin.

"You all right?" I started in. "Lost a fiver? Had to buy someone a drink?" He looked at me for a moment. "Good luck," he said quietly, gesturing inwards with his head. Not very encouraging.

Psyche looked apprehensive and even paler than usual. I started to feel a lot less confident. On the way to the cinema she seemed depressed and spoke in a low voice.

I trust the diary at this point.

She piloted me into a seat well forward of the back row. Fair enough, I didn't intend trying to ravish her in the Kensington Odeon, but she sat right on the far side of her seat from me. I waited, but when I attempted an affectionate move, she didn't respond. I left it at that.

After the cinema, we went round to Jeanie's house. Tony and Johnny were there. They were closely involved, to put it politely, with members of the opposite sex. The lights were so low as to be almost unlit. I fetched drinks and Psyche made a point of sitting on a chair made for one. I got her to sit close by me and asked her what was happening, what was wrong, pressing her, I suppose, quite hard. All around us we could hear lips on lips, hands rustling and swishing through garments, little groans and sighs.

Eventually she admitted she didn't like "necking." I said the current environment was perhaps a bit warm, as it were, and maybe we should just go for a stroll. She looked down and shook her head. I felt hollow but I had to push it. I asked if her dislike of necking was necking with anyone, or just with me. She said something about thinking I was the right person last week, but now knowing she had made a mistake.

At this point, mercifully, I didn't write about my feelings. I do remember a new sensation: dead inside, remote from my surroundings. A kind of emotional shock reaction, I guess. Later, on the way home, all the feelings you'd expect swarmed over me.

A kind of helpless rage: how could she lead me on like that? Then a useless justification: I treated her considerately and gently, so it must be her, she's just too strange. A desperate insecurity: it's class, she's out of my reach, she's used to wealth, I was aiming too high. And finally, a desolate sadness. I was surprised to find it lasted for days. "Perhaps I'm not as trivial and glib as I thought I was," I said to myself, with a futile sort of inverted pride.

But at the time, in that sweaty room, after an immeasurable silence, I managed, "I'm the same person tonight as I was last week. It was only a few days ago."

Another lengthy silence. I saw she was actually trembling a little and I realised that this environment, with what people used to call "heavy petting" all round us, must feel oppressive to her.

"Look, at least let me walk you home. I'll keep a yard away at all times, honest."

My pained joke didn't go well. She gave an odd little gasp and started weeping.

"Oh, come on, let's get out of here."

I took her hand and led her out on to the pavement. She seemed to have lost all willpower. She didn't withdraw her hand and I simply led her back to the flat.

In George's living room, I sat her down and stood over her. "Look, I'll clear off now. Will you be okay?" She didn't look up, just a couple of little nods. I was completely baffled. I wanted to take her in my arms and soothe her, I wanted to shout at her, I wanted...I didn't know what.

"Maybe I'll give you a ring just to see how you are, no more. Okay?"

I couldn't bear to think I'd never see her again. I looked down at her neck, helplessly, and turned to walk out. The door burst open and Tony came in. His face was tense.

"Gerry, please don't go. Psyche, we need to talk to him."

He sat down opposite us.

"Thing is, Gerry, this has happened before, and fairly recently, fairly often, in fact. You've got some sort of barrier about going out with boys, haven't you, Psyche?"

"So Tony, why tell me I was in with a chance?"

Psyche looked up and spoke quietly but firmly. "You had no right to do that, Tony."

Tony's answer washed away my resentment.

"Because I think you are sensitive and careful enough to help her live more fully...and I do want my big sister to enjoy her life. Even though you look like the back end of a bus, it might have worked."

Psyche didn't laugh at his little joke, but then, nor did I.

I could see her looking for words, starting to speak, then the tears.

"I made a mistake, I'm sorry, I feel awful," that sort of thing would have helped me, and maybe her too. But no such words came.

She sat almost silent, except for, very quietly, "I just have this thing about boys," then the weeping started again, shuddering sobs this time. She was like a different person, leaning forward head in hands, a different girl from the one who put her head on my shoulder a few days before. I was tired of looking at the top of her head, so I knelt on the carpet, lifted her chin and looked into her face. I had to keep a grip on myself.

"Come on, Psyche, life goes on." Such a platitude. "Can I give you a ring to see how you are?" The gulps eased off and she nodded glumly. I left in tears neither of them could have seen.

In the diary a few days later:

She reads a lot, loses herself in music, partly because she is scared of facing up to real life, scared of how much it hurts sometimes to be really alive, yet she is sensitive enough to know and understand what it means to live a full life.

I knew little enough about a full life at that age and anyway they were the words of a young hypocrite. Lead a full life with me is what I meant and that life would include a double bed.

George's flat was too interesting a place and Tony was too close a friend for me to disappear. I think I was a little in love with all of them, up there on the third floor in their Floating World, but most of all, despite giving myself a good talking-to, I was in love with Psyche. I realised this hadn't happened before, it was a new big thing, at 18. I decided it was true what they said. It wasn't easy.

I visited the flat a few times more that September. We'd be round there with friends from The Elephant and Psyche would slip in and out, looking tense. Tony had relaxed, now he thought his valiant effort had failed. He thought I had got over it. Well, one doesn't tell all the truth of one's heart, even to one's best friend, now does one? This one didn't, anyway.

Sometimes George would glide in, trailing a star or two. It might be a young singer or musician from Psyche's school, or a celebrated choreographer. It might be a composer. George was careful to introduce his stars in passing. I felt grateful to be there, despite a recurrent sharp ache when I saw Psyche drift past. One evening, when I arrived on my own, I was embarrassed to find that he'd been having a dinner party and the guests were just leaving. "Oh, I'm sorry George, I'll clear off."

"No don't," he replied, "I'm chucking this lot out anyway."

"This lot" included Bill Evans.

Over their shoulders, I saw Psyche disappearing into another room. She must have heard my voice. But jazz was a passion of hers, which I learned later that evening when Tony lured her out of her room and sat us down with a drink.

"For fuck's sake, talk to each other," he commanded, as I gazed at her helplessly and she looked at the carpet.

"Don't use language like that in front of your" swallowing hard and noisily "beautiful older sister, you yob."

Psyche delivered herself of a couple of sentences at this point. "It doesn't help paying me compliments Gerry." Long pause. "I feel so ashamed."

Tony started to say something, but I held my palm up to him, without taking my eyes off her face.

"There's no point in feeling ashamed. It won't help you or me."

She looked up. "I know, I know."

Long pause. Her head went down again. I looked helplessly at Tony. He shrugged, also helplessly. I thought perhaps I should go, but I didn't want to. Still wanted to look at her, even if it was only the top of her head. Ridiculous. I said, slightly desperately, "Was that Bill Evans who just left? THE Bill Evans, the greatest jazz pianist in the world?"

At last she sat back in her chair and looked at me. A result. Thanks, Bill.

"You like his music?"

We had a pleasant enough chat about jazz. She was right up with the latest sounds, even played some on George's beautiful hifi. It was not unheard of, but still quite unusual back then, to find girls who liked modern jazz.

George came in whilst we were playing "Undercurrent," Bill Evans and Jim Hall, gentle healing sounds. At least, so I hoped. "Romain," "Skating in Central Park," "Darn that Dream."

"Ah, Mr Evans. He's playing Ronnie's. Would you like to go and see him, Gerry?"

I very much absolutely definitely would.

"How about you, Psyche? Gerry can squire you safely through Soho, he's such a gent."

Oh, myriad blessings on your head, George. She looked very anxious, flicked a glance at me. I said "It'll be okay," and I think she knew what I meant: hands off. She said yes, she would like to go. George said we were to leave it to him.

It would be hell to keep my distance from Psyche for a long and late evening but – Bill Evans! Psyche went to her room soon after this sort-of-date was fixed up. Tony said quietly "Well done, you shifty little git. It might help." As I turned to go, George was at my shoulder. George didn't walk up to you, he materialised silently beside you.

"Got a moment?"

Of course I had and I thanked him profusely. Scott's was sold out for Bill Evans' run and Scott's wasn't cheap. I was genuinely grateful. He held up a hand to stop me.

"I want to thank you for agreeing to take my daughter to Ronnie's. Probably old-fashioned of me but Soho late at night is not a place for a girl on her own and she will love the gig. She needs something to lift her spirits."

He looked thoughtfully at me and I began to splutter a bit.

"It's okay. Tony's filled me in. I hope she doesn't hurt you. She doesn't mean to. She can't help it. I'm quite worried about her."

What to say? I wasn't used to this sort of confidence from a sophisticated adult.

"Well, George, I'll do what I can, she's...she's such a lovely girl...I mean...in so many ways..."

Stop digging, as we'd say these days. George looked at me for a moment, nodded once and vanished as silently as usual.

The Bill Evans gig. If you don't know his music, the next bit may not mean anything much to you. He sat with his nose almost on the keyboard, hardly spoke to us, nodded once or twice when we applauded. His face was a sort of grey-green colour, probably due to the latest stage of his addictions. And the music just poured over us. It sounded as though he'd composed it beforehand, such crystalline beauty, yet he could also swing like the clappers. Psyche's face shone. I began to feel a little healed.

In its way, the evening was a success. Watching Psyche in Ronnie's and talking jazz on the way back to George's was more of a delight than I'd expected. It was late when we got back, so I waited till she had the front door open, then darted up to her, took her hand and kissed it with a mock-gallant flourish. She actually giggled, and hurried into the house.

I thought perhaps Psyche and I were on a relatively even keel after the evening at Scott's. I couldn't get up to George's for a while, had to work and get ready for university. I thought I should nip up there before I left and say cheerio, until the Christmas holidays. And I still hoped for more from Psyche, of course I did.

But really, I said to myself, you're just dropping by to say cheerio. Nice and casual – Light touch. Maybe leave something there to flower over Christmas, who knows? How grown-up.

I walked into the flat. Tony, who thought I was over his sister, introduced me to a young man called Martin. Psyche glided in, said "Hi" to me, trying hard to sound nonchalant, "have a good term," put her arm through Martin's and drifted out, past me and what I hoped was a stony glare.

I stared at the door. I was burning with anger, full of shame at having exposed what I thought was my tender side, bitterly disappointed. Tony watched my face.

"Ah. I see. Oh dear. The flame still burns."

"Well it was doing," I almost yelled at him, "but it's just gone out. Been pissed on. It appears it's not boys she is hung up about, it's me. Some honesty would have helped. I feel such a fucking idiot. Is your sister just a prick-teaser or what is going on?"

He'd not got angry with me before. It was level and quiet and unpleasantly cold.

"Don't you ever talk about her like that again. I thought you cared for her, wanted to help her. Perhaps you were just trying to get her into bed." This was undeniably true but there was more to it than that.

We stared at each other. Impasse. But I was damned if I'd let my feelings for Psyche ruin my friendship with her brother.

"I'm sorry, Tony, I apologise. I just don't understand her."

"Do you think we do?" came George's calm voice from across the room. "You're a nice boy, Gerry, go home and forget her. We'll help her along as best we can. Least said, soonest mended and all that. She can't help being beautiful and she doesn't know what to do with it."

She seemed to know what to do with it this evening, I thought. George added: "And Martin is also a nice boy, so don't worry about her. Let go."

I wanted to devise twenty ways of putting Martin to death but I owed George a response.

"I'm sorry, George, really I am. I'm just a hopeless romantic. I need to grow up. I hope she'll be okay. You've all been very kind and generous and I think I'd better leave now."

"Come and see us in the Christmas vacation, if you feel like it." He went into the next room and I left. I went home and put "Darn That Dream" on the hi-fi.

Chapter Five

Liverpool

I tried to darn that dream. I didn't go near the flat for many months, though I did hitch down to London, to visit Scott's and see some of the Elephant and Castle crowd.

"What are you doing here?" yelled Johnny across a crowded bar. "Come to sniff around Tony's sister?"

"Shut up Johnny, if you still want any front teeth." An empty boast, as he well knew, but my intensity startled him.

"Oh, calm down, lover boy. What are you drinking?"

Who was it at Scott's? Maybe Ben Webster. It was a great evening, but it wasn't transcendent, wasn't Evans the Jazz. It lacked Psyche.

I remember walking London's wet autumnal streets, leaves swirling down from the plane trees, cars swishing past. I've always enjoyed finding a song to match a mood and a season and this time it was Dinah Washington, "September in the Rain." It seemed elegiac, calling back to something that felt as though it had happened quite a while ago because so much was going on in Liverpool. I decided I really was getting over Psyche, or getting past her. She was back then and back there, I was here and now. I felt different, in Liverpool. But then young people often misjudge the power of the past, particularly when it's their own past.

After the trip to Scott's, the journey back to Liverpool was long and tedious. It was good to be back in this new world, new friends, new city. The Beatles had left the city by then but there was a backwash of pleasant nostalgia, nostalgia for all of two years earlier. Parties were full of "A Hard Day's Night" and those songs still have a strong pull for me. It was to the sound of that album that I managed at last to get rid of my virginity: hallelujah! The earth didn't exactly move. She was a nice girl, brisk, and surprisingly business-like. Fortunately, she was more experienced than I was.

"Hey, slow down! Take your time, there's no rush…"

She had dark hair and a pale face, though she wasn't particularly tall and graceful, so I wasn't looking for a second Psyche, was I? We tried a few weeks' chatting plus quite a lot more of her business-like tuition. I was grateful to her but I knew I mustn't mislead her, I knew we weren't going anywhere.

"No big deal," she said, "we don't have to be going anywhere, we just need to enjoy it, you know?" Thanks to her, I did. And we stayed friends, still are friends. Thank you, Jenny.

I suppose it was "the sixties," a time of "free" love, the blessings of The Pill. But those sixties had hardly arrived by early 1965. People are probably thinking of '66-'70 when they generalise about the decade. And anyway, free love was a lot freer for men than women who, as far as I remember, got dropped and left rather more often than vice versa and still had to worry about falling pregnant.

Many boys of my generation were still sexually inexperienced by the time they went to college. Perhaps that made us more inclined to romanticise and idealise, but underneath the romance, male cultures were by modern standards often crude and degrading. The double standard was far from dead. "The college bike" was always a girl, never a man. "She goes like a steam train." How pleased "she" would have been to know that. But then, some aspects of sex in our culture that are commonplace nowadays would have disturbed and scared us back then.

In my early adolescence, we were still dominated by models of restraint, longing and inhibition, which generated a kind of super-charged furtiveness. Maybe that's what made us – well, me, anyway – romantic and fantastical, compared with people a little younger than me. Jenny started me on a calm and sensible course through these exciting, risky times. But it was only a start.

The wide Mersey, ferries still running, ships still in dock. The damp, salty wind off the water, bohemian and grubby Liverpool 8, gentrified and cleaned up beyond recognition these days. The verbal vigour of Scousers. The ornate splendour of the Philharmonic Rooms, "the Phil" Draught Guinness at "The Crack," noisy and friendly. The city had a powerful identity. These were high times for me. The glamorous world of George's flat, with his beautiful daughter as the melancholy spirit of the place, all that seemed long ago and far away.

Tony had got into Cambridge, as I'd felt sure he would. We exchanged letters a couple of times. He didn't mention his sister – kindness? embarrassment? So nor did I. He complained that I hadn't been to see them over Christmas. I made an excuse, but I'd taken George's advice and moved on. And I had met Bethan.

She was quite short, had brown hair, a cheerful round lightly freckled face and a figure that just made me want to cuddle her. I saw this as a sign that any remaining spell around black hair and a pale face was broken. She was very different from Psyche. She was Welsh, non-metropolitan, direct, with a dangerous sense of humour, which often started with a wrinkling of her turned-up little nose. She never hesitated to mock my cultural pretensions, though she couldn't get near my cricket, which I carried forward from school into the university teams. She hated jazz, loved beat music (such a silly term) and ignored classical music.

"It's got no words and it goes on and on. Boring!"

"It's not boring, it's Miles Davis."

The nose began to wrinkle.

"Well, it misses me by miles, anyway."

She grinned. "Take me to The Sink and we'll have some real lovely music!"

"It's full of mods."

"Let's be mods for an evening then. Come on!"

Impossible, delightful girl.

On an evening early in our relationship, in my room, we found we needed to tear the clothes off each other and set to for the first time. I didn't have any condoms. In a panic I terminated proceedings abruptly, and deposited my dangerously reproductive offering across her belly. She was startled for a moment, then she laughed.

"You don't have to do that, you silly boy. You could've stayed put. I'm on the pill."

"I thought the pill was only for married women?"

"Ah well, there you are, then," she said. "I'll let you into a secret. My dad's a doctor. But you are not to tell anyone, he'd get into big trouble." Semi-serious now, I swore his secret would die with me.

Thus did I begin to grow up a little.

Bethan's father was not only a doctor, he was a dry old stick. Bethan had inherited his sharp wit but she also had a sense of fun, which as far as I could see was entirely lacking in her father. Adults in 1965 didn't always react warmly to the sense of irresponsible freedom that came off my generation like steam off a sweaty horse in the sunshine. On my first visit to Colwyn Bay, Doctor Jennings asked me pointedly what I wanted to do with the rest of my life after I'd graduated.

"I don't know," I said, "maybe live in a Scottish croft, grow spuds and write a best-seller?"

He took me seriously. "All three of those objectives would be difficult to achieve. How would you actually earn a living?"

I was going off him rapidly.

"I really don't know, at this stage."

"What is your field of study?"

I wanted to say: your daughter, with particular reference to her sweet little body.

"History. With English. And some philosophy."

"I see," replied the Good Doctor, unimpressed, and turned away to assist with laying the dinner table. Bethan looked downcast. I winked at her. It didn't help. When we were alone, I said "Bethan, he's talking as if I had asked for permission to marry you."

Bethan wriggled in her chair and looked down.

"He may think that's why you're here. The Pill, you see. He can just about accept living together before marriage, with the Pill as a safeguard, provided it's...well, you know, it's on the way to marriage and the whole thing."

I suddenly felt trapped, which wasn't fair, but then neither of us was in the formal "it's time to meet my parents" mode. We'd more or less dropped in at the last minute. Bethan wanted to show me something of Wales and we'd hitched to Colwyn Bay. Dr and Mrs Jennings were pleased to see their girl and they welcomed me on arrival, as good hosts do. But it all began to feel a little forensic.

Over dinner, the usefulness or otherwise of a degree in history and English was scrutinised. Bethan's mother was encouraging and asked me what I thought my career route might be, if I got a good degree.

Since I didn't have any career route in mind just then apart from enjoying myself, I had to improvise. I told them the civil service was an option, or journalism, the BBC, that sort of thing.

"Teaching?" she asked. I sensed a likely question about serving others. "Well, maybe, but probably not in universities."

"But to be direct," said the Good Doctor, not that he was ever anything else, "what use is history, to the general good?"

That was an easy one. "Right. Two points, Doctor Jennings. If we don't learn from the mistakes of history we are doomed to repeat them. Secondly, a society without a sense of its history is like a man without a memory; neither knows where they have come from. Welsh people might find that a particularly strong argument."

"Maybe so, but I'm not Welsh." I looked, puzzled, at Bethan, who muttered "I was born here, Dad wasn't."

"Those are fluent answers," he added.

He watched me a little longer. I smiled back at him. He obviously thought I was full of bullshit and he may have been right, because he then asked a little too sharply "and who first made those two points, may I ask? You?"

"No. I've no idea where they come from, they are useful, though."

I'd had almost enough of this, so I added "They make sense to me, and I got them from a lecturer in Liverpool University."

"Well, they sound good, but I'm not sure they have any empirical basis," said the Good Doctor.

"Empirical basis? Well, history isn't a science, but it is different from fiction, you know."

"I'm relieved to hear it," was his parting shot.

Mrs Jennings slid in pleasantly and easily. I guessed she was used to it.

"Is Liverpool a good university for history, do you think? Are you enjoying your studies?"

"Well, they took me on, so clearly it's a good university now." Bethan spluttered into her coffee.

"And yes, thanks, I am enjoying the course so far."

Oh sod it. Now the Good Doctor thought I was a clever-dick as well as fluently superficial.

I was in the guest room. I hadn't expected anything else. We weren't in Sweden, that mythical land of sexual free-for-all, but I was interested by the idea of a doctor who would break the law to put his daughter on the pill but then refuse her a chance to put that pill to good use. Under his own roof, at least.

The next morning quite early Bethan brought me a cup of tea in bed. I had expected a little pleasant misbehaviour when she walked in, but she sat down on the end of the bed and watched me.

"I expect you think Dad doesn't like you."

I was startled.

"I've no idea. He presses a bit hard. He probably thinks I'm too flippant for my own good. Maybe yours too." I suddenly felt despondent. "Maybe he's right."

"Maybe he bloody well isn't," she snapped.

I stared at her.

"Thing is, see, he was an army doctor in the war and he saw some dreadful things. In Burma. Mum says he won't talk about it, but it's not made him very tolerant, and he's anxious on my behalf. But I'll make my own way, he needs to ease off."

"Look, don't worry. Let's leave them in peace. Shall we go back to Liverpool?"

"I want to show you the mountains and the beaches. Mum says she'll drive us."

That was kind. It wasn't raining much and I was greatly taken by Snowdonia and the beaches of Anglesey, with their views of distant mountains. I'd never actually seen a mountain before.

"Typical bloody Southerner!" Bethan said.

Her mother was a careful driver and we got back to Colwyn Bay in the middle of the evening. I rather dreaded another cross-examination from the Good Doctor but he was out visiting patients. I'm sure he was a good doctor and maybe not as stern as he made out. And Bethan was an only child, after all.

"It's getting late, how about fish and chips?" said Mrs Jennings, and we had a jollier sort of evening. Poor Dr Jennings. I wonder if people often heaved a sigh of relief when his demanding, serious-minded presence left the room.

We left the next day "for the station," we lied, so sparing them anxiety and us the embarrassment of a direct lie. Bethan's mother was kindly and gave us affectionate goodbyes.

"Don't take my husband too seriously, Gerald," she said. "He's actually quite shy and his bark is worse than his bite." She pronounced "bark" as in JS Bach.

"Mummy's favourite little joke," Bethan explained. "Dad's actually a good amateur pianist, isn't he, Mum?"

"Did he woo you with partitas and sweep you off your feet with toccatas, Mrs Jennings?"

Bit risky, but she liked it, and even blushed a little. "Ah, that would be telling," she said and gave me a little peck on my cheek as we left.

"Naughty boy," Bethan muttered with a grin, and took my hand.

Over the next few days, my mind kept going back to the idea that the Good Doctor had essentially been quizzing a prospective son-in-law. Surely not, I told myself. Mrs Jennings showed no signs of hearing wedding bells in the breeze and she mentioned on our drive that she felt modern enough to think that a little experience of life during student days was "probably a good thing, before settling down."

Settling down. I had no sense of that, no sense of how that could even happen to me. It wasn't fair on Bethan but I did feel more constrained than before our trip to Colwyn. I watched to see if she was thinking of settling down, but I saw no such signs.

Chapter Six

Transition

When I arrived at Liverpool University, students looked more or less like any young adult. My older contemporaries still wore a college scarf sometimes, and duffle coats could still be seen. The only drugs around, in my circle at least, were fags and alcohol, those two killers. As 1965 wore on, the duffel coats disappeared and the scarves were mostly used for hitchhiking. Hair got just a little longer. My leather jacket looked less distinctive, to my disappointment. The Beatles released "Rubber Soul," which sounded very new and truly distinctive. The Stones got wilder. The Who arrived a lot wilder towards the end of the year. Mod fashions were to be seen around town. And a few of us began smoking dope, easier to find in a port city than in a London suburb.

After I got home for Easter, Tony and I spoke on the phone a couple of times, still not mentioning Psyche, which was okay by me. He sounded different on the phone. Slightly amplified, a little slower in his responses. We arranged to meet at The Elephant. He said he wanted to tell me some big news.

It was great to meet up with him again. Blokes didn't hug much back then. Had it been nowadays, we certainly would have done. He looked different, perhaps a little strained round the eyes, but perhaps he was just tired. Couldn't put my finger on it. But then it had been six or seven months since we'd met. At school, we'd seen each other every day. The usual piss-taking ensued about whose round it was and we settled in a corner.

It was quite early and the pub was quiet. Tony launched straight in.

"How's university? I've jacked it in. I bet you've already learned all you'll ever learn from them."

I was astonished.

"Why on earth have you left, Tony? Are you okay? How's George about it?"

"I'm fine. Dad says it's up to me but I'll need a job and he says he'll help me find one."

"Didn't you like Cambridge? Why leave?"

"Same reason you should leave Liverpool. Universities are institutions designed to prevent liberation. They reek of past confusions, they encourage contradictions within us."

These were strange statements. He was waiting for my response.

"Well, I really like life in Liverpool, the course is mostly fine, good friends, lively times."

"You're so good at seeing the best in dull things, Gerry."

That shook me a bit.

"Nothing ordinary about life up there, for me. Look, why not give Cambridge another try? Maths at Cambridge, come on..."

He clearly wasn't going to go back. We argued half-heartedly around the point, which was in fact pointless. He'd moved on, but to what?

"I feel sad about that, you're a clever little twat and a degree from Cambridge could lead to something good."

"To what? More of the same? I am re-making myself, or rather I am being re-made. By The Transition."

I could hear the capital letters but the name was meaningless. This was getting very strange. I just stared at him for a moment.

"You think I'm off my head. Don't you?"

He looked fierce. Time to lighten the mood.

"Perhaps oui, perhaps non, mon ami. Mais c'est quoi, çe Transition?" This was a throwback to a daft quasi-French silly accents game at school. He didn't smile. I could see he'd moved on further and faster from Dallinghoo than I had. He looked round. The pub was filling up and getting noisier.

"Look, finish your drink. Let's walk. Then I'll drive you to Waterloo."

He had hardly touched his pint, although I'd bought it for him. He stood up.

"Unless you want to come round to the flat and see Psyche." This was neutrally and carefully said, but it still smarted a little.

"It's okay Tony, I've taken George's advice. Anyway, I don't want to bump into her and Martin again."

He laughed. It sounded almost callous.

"Oh, that didn't last long. No one has, you must have guessed that. But look. I don't want to talk about my sister's hang-ups, I want to talk about me. And you're fucking well going to listen, bonehead!"

This was more like the old Tony. I was encouraged, but as we wandered around Kensington, that encouragement didn't last long. I really tried to listen to him, but it was confusing stuff.

"So what's the point of these 'target point' things?"

"That's simply what you get set. You have to work yourself clear of anything that contradicts your perception. It's resolving contradictions. You see, Gerry, what I'm doing is scraping myself right down to the basic spiritual truth, and then rebuilding myself into a fully liberated person, holy and unique."

"What?"

I'd thought we were just going for a pint and a catch-up. Spiritual truth, from a mathematics Exhibitioner at Cambridge? A holy and unique person? Stone me, as Hancock used to say.

"Tony, you're leaving me behind, I don't – "

"I'm at a very exciting point, close to breakthrough. I'm due to leave quite soon for abroad, the Caribbean or Mexico maybe, with the group. I don't know when I'll next see you. And...I'm having trouble raising all the cash. So, mon vieux...any chance you could lend me a tenner?"

That did make me stare.

"Isn't George backing you? He's always been so supportive."

"I haven't told him, or Psyche. In fact, it's a deadly secret. Don't tell anyone, or I shall have to kill you."

I was beginning to think that he half meant it, he was so elsewhere, so out of his head. He grinned.

"I'm not in the habit of murdering my best friends, though I could make an exception if you don't keep schtum."

It was very confusing to see the old, everyday Tony emerging through the strange new jargon and then vanishing behind it again.

We were quite close to the flat by now.

"Here's the car. Hop in."

It was a Mini-Cooper and I endured the most frightening journey of my life. He cut up the traffic, ignoring horns and gestures, accelerated hard up to traffic lights, scorched away from them and hit 60 in a 40 limit.

"Christsake slow down, Tony, I'm scared."

"Relax. You know that thunderstorm last night? It was when I hit my final target point. That's no coincidence. You're safe with me. I'm untouchable."

"Well I'm not," I yelled.

"I'm a fully realised Transition member and my life has never felt so good."

"Then fuck's sake prolong it a little. And mine too. PLEASE."

I was pretty shaken up when he dropped me off at Waterloo.

"Tony, please don't drive like that. You'll get nicked for sure. Here's your tenner. You'll need it for the fine you'll get."

Big grin.

"Anyway, where'd you get this motor? Thought you were broke."

"I am. It's not mine. I borrowed it. Gotta get it back now."

"Look, keep in touch, tell me how you get on."

I felt like pleading with him. I wanted him back, and I could feel him going from me.

Another grin through the open car window.

"Relax, Gerry. Our paths are determined by our freedom from compulsions. Get into The Transition and you'll see what I mean."

The Mini-Cooper roared away from the kerb. I felt sure the owner of that hot little car didn't know it had been borrowed.

I've still got a few letters from Tony. One was written soon after he left me shaken at Waterloo Station.

"Gerald, get yourself out of Liverpool University and into The Transition. Don't waste time, don't hum and ha, you sluggish slug. Just do it. Liberate yourself!" and then lots of jargon-blasted stuff about compulsions and targets and sessions with a meter. Just as that evening in The Elephant, he surfaced briefly, sounding like the Tony I knew so well, and then dived back under the surface scum again. I got really alarmed by stuff like this:

"Gerry, I can understand your misgivings. I was anxious at first. But the latest development puts this thing beyond doubt. We've been meditating together and asking questions, big questions. In response, one or two of us have been contacted by something beyond this life. We call it The Beyond. We've tried out various questions and we can trust it. YOU can trust it, Gerry. It's The Beyond that convinced us we should go west, to the Caribbean."

If I had ever thought that aspects of The Transition were interesting and worthwhile as psychotherapy, this sort of stuff killed it off. My anxiety for Tony rose even higher. Should I tell George about all this? About the big trip being planned? But maybe I was over-reacting, just because my friend had changed so much. People change...

Back in Liverpool, I tried to let my worries fade. Bethan was very helpful and very firm. Her sweet round face was troubled, her brow drawn into a frown.

"Don't go near it. They're mad, bonkers."

I didn't think Tony was actually mad, but he certainly wasn't making much sense.

"What worries me is that he's just not the same."

"He's changed. Like people do. And you're not the same as him anyway, so stand back, Gerry, I think it's dangerous."

"What should I do, then?"

"Nothing. What can you do? He'll do what he wants. Come on, cariad, cheer up," she said, pressing herself against me, which worked, as it usually did.

University life rolled on round me, sweeping me along, leaving Tony's Transition in its wake. My cricket season was going well. Then back in Hall one evening, I was called down to the public phone by the front door.

"Some posh Southern bird for you, mate. T'ent Bethan."

Indeed not. I knew the voice at once.

"Gerry?" A big intake of breath then a pause. I waited.

"I need your help."

I sighed and she must have heard it. "I wouldn't have phoned you if it wasn't really important. I'm sorry, so sorry about everything, but – "

I cut across her: "Hello, Psyche."

I was surprised at how pleased I was to hear her voice.

"What is it?"

"It's Tony. And George."

She never called him "Dad," as Tony did.

"I don't know what to do."

"Tell me more."

"I can't, one of them will come back in soon. Can you come down?" Her voice was shaky. "As if it was by chance. Just drop in. Soon. Please."

I paused. Cricket match this weekend, date with Bethan for a party or two...but Psyche's voice was shaky. My voice answered, though I wasn't sure where it came from.

"I'll be down Friday evening."

The first team captain was furious. I fended him off.

"I just don't feel up to it. And look - when did I miss a match or not do my best?" He sulked, but got over it after a week or two. Our team won in my absence, which helped him but not me.

Bethan was furious and intensely suspicious. "Tell me MORE. I don't understand. She isn't a girlfriend, she wasn't ever a girlfriend, you don't know her very well...you'll write off the weekend for her?"

"No. Not for her. For Tony."

I doubted myself. Why was I playing the knight on a big white charger riding to the rescue of the girl who had chucked me? Well, I told myself, I wasn't. I just wanted to help Tony. Of course that was it. And that's what I told Bethan. And she kind of accepted it in the end. I thought.

The familiar door, the familiar bell. Psyche opened the door, and her eyes widened, and filled. She was wearing a white polo-neck jersey and black jeans. I stared back, at all of her. O God, I thought, here we go again...

She spoke very quietly, even for her.

"Oh thank you, thank you."

Impulsively, I reached forward and held my index finger gently against her lips. I felt something like a tiny electric charge.

"Sshh," was all I said.

She spun round and tried to crank up some surprised delight to whoever was in the room. She was trying too hard and it sounded thin.

"Now look who's just rolled up, out of the blue."

Again, I said "sshh" so only she could hear. She stepped aside and there were George and Tony opposite each other at a table. Tony looked fierce and drawn. He glared at me.

"Out of the blue, my arse," he said harshly.

"Good to see you too, Tony," I said, trying to keep it calm. I took Psyche's hand, squeezed it and walked towards them. George was, or seemed, as calm as ever.

"Good evening, Gerry, how's Liverpool?"

"Fine thanks George but I fancied a little London weekend life and I thought I'd drop by, haven't seen any of you for so long."

"She set you up. I've been set up." But Tony looked less certain now. My story sounded plausible even to me, and Psyche had her own reasons for looking a little tense when she saw me again. We might just about be able to hide her little plot from him.

"If this is difficult, George, I can clear off."

"I'm pleased to see you, Gerry, and Tony will be too when he steadies up and drops his persecution mania. Let's have a drink and sit on the sofas, this is too confrontational."

We talked for a couple of hours.

"I understand that Tony has found a set of beliefs he finds helpful," George said, "beliefs he can identify with. It doesn't matter if I, or any of us, or any of Tony's old friends, don't share those beliefs."

"What do you know about it all, George?"

"I've been to see the man who runs everything. I think..." he paused, looking for the right words, not wanting to alienate his son.

"I think he is an interesting and impressive person. I'm sorry Tony, but I'm not sure I trust him. He seems to have a powerful hold on his followers. That's what worries me."

A small explosion from Tony at this point.

"Dad, dad. It's not you who has to trust him, that's not fair. You –
"

George interrupted him, which was unusual for him.

"Tony, Gerry asked me how much I knew about it all. I'm just trying to answer his question." Calm as ever.

Psyche sat leaning forward with her head down, dark hair hiding her face. Tony turned abruptly to her.

"You said you were interested, you said you might join us."

Quietly, from inside the hair, "That was when it was psychotherapy. Now it's a strange kind of religion and they frighten me."

Tony calmed abruptly. "Well, I can understand that. But communication with The Beyond came from our united meditations, we didn't just dream it up. Terry channels it for us, of course."

"Of course? Oh yes, of course he does, he controls it all," looking up at her brother suddenly, "they are taking you over, Tony, can't you see that?"

Tony sighed.

"Look, sister, what do you know? You only came to one or two sessions."

So she'd tried it too. I looked across at George, who raised his eyebrows at the news.

Tony went on. "You'd learn so much, Gerry, if you came along too. Perhaps you could bring Psyche."

"That's okay," I said, trying my favourite but frequently useless light touch, "I'll stick with cricket. That's enough of a religion for me." Which earned a snort of derision from Tony.

George asked his son to explain again, in front of the three of us, why he felt it was so helpful. Tony gave us quite a speech.

"The therapy makes you break down the compulsions and illusions we all build up, so that eventually you are left with your own one true identity, the single power that drives each of us, if only we can find it and free it. Once you have found it, you are new made, a free man. You can see where you are in your life and how to live it. Each person's single power relates to a spiritual identity, an actual spirit. That's why each member is given a new name, to symbolise the powerful, free person."

It was all very clear – to him.

"What in particular worries you about all this, George?" I asked, playing neutral chairman.

George looked at me for a moment. I wondered how much he knew of Tony's plans, but he then told me something I hadn't known.

"Tony was on TV last night. Look." He passed over the Evening Standard, folded back so I could see the story. Tony and Johnny Walker, who was now also a Transition member, had been aggressive and rude to a well-respected journalist who was trying to interview them.

I looked up from the paper. Tony was watching for my reaction. The story didn't read well for him. I kept my neutral face.

All Tony said was, "He had it coming."

"Why?"

"He refused to accept the reality of what we were telling him."

"So might I. Would you be cross and rude to anyone who didn't follow this Transition?"

"Quite possibly, especially if they were hostile about us."

George sighed. "Did you read the whole story, Gerry? Did you notice anything extraordinary?"

I tried not to squirm. "Well, it says they are all going to the Caribbean, to live together communally and refine The Transition."

George said, "When would you have told us, Gerry?"

How did he know I already knew? Could I be read so easily? Probably, yes.

"Tony made me promise not to tell you, or anyone."

"A moral problem for you."

Quietly but intensely, from Psyche:

"It's not Gerry's fault his best friend is going off the rails." She kept her head down; we waited for Tony's response. He stared at me, and surprised me with: "Thank you for keeping your word, Gerry. And you're right, Psyche. I am going off the rails that drive us further and further into confusion, into meaningless, trivial, violent chaos." His voice was rising. Time to intervene.

"How will you live out there?"

"Simply."

It felt like a rebuke. I felt resentful and confused. Why was I sitting here? Tony's mad Transition had nothing to do with me. I was just trying to be kind to Psyche, and support my newly weird friend. But maybe my confusion actually supported some of the things Tony had been saying? Bloody hell.

"George, I could do with a top-up, if that's okay."

"Help yourself, and us too, please"

George looked remote, brooding, as I handed him his drink. We all kept quiet for a few moments.

He came back to life, and spoke slowly, carefully, and at surprising length.

"The basics are this. Tony feels he is finding a new purpose in his life. His sister and I worry that even if he is, he is doing so at the beck and call of a very dominant person. Sensitive intelligent young people, such as all three of you, tend to look for clear meanings, a definite direction, to help them grow into the next stage of their lives. Tony has found a direction. Okay so far?"

Nods from Psyche and me, nothing from Tony

"But...it's not one I'm happy with, and in particular, I am completely opposed to Tony going to the Caribbean. He would be one of the youngest in the group, he's still well under 21. I could have him legally prevented from going and if he persists, I shall have to do so. In Mexico, or wherever they land up, he would be under the control of people I know almost nothing about and the little I do know troubles me deeply. How could I live the rest of my life if I allowed him to be endangered, mentally or physically?"

I found George's thinking irrefutable and I was relieved by his level, calm manner. But this was the moment when Tony gave up trying to keep his father and his sister in touch with his Transition. I could see the resignation in his face.

"Well I'm sorry, Dad, I'm going to bed."

He looked miserable and defiant. I felt profoundly saddened.

Psyche was crying quietly. Tony got up and left the room.

George brooded some more, then he said "He's lucky having a sister and a pal like you two. I know you'll do what you can. You're welcome to kip down here if you like, Gerry, it's getting late."

He got up and drifted off. Psyche disappeared to fetch bedding for the sofa and I fished out some overnight stuff from my bag. Back on the old sofa again, but so much had changed round me since I last slept on it. The tension in the room had been insistent. I felt drained, and was already half asleep when Psyche threw a duvet over me and disappeared.

I woke in the dawn light and thought about the previous evening, before drifting off again. I woke later with a start. There was a face just a few inches from mine. It kissed me very lightly – cheeks, forehead. I lay astonished, passive. I closed my eyes and they received two very gentle kisses too.

"Thank you so very much," said Psyche. She sat on the floor beside the sofa, reached for my hand and held it.

"Psyche," I croaked, "could we have some tea, and a chat?"

Tony wrote to Johnny Walker after the discussion with his sister, his father and me:

I must not get angry. Terry and the others would tell me that anger's a distraction, a contradiction of my one direction. It will keep me away from the Beyond.

It's not their fault. Gerry's always been more cautious than me, he was so at school. So straight, so daily stuff in front of you dah de dah de dah dah dah.

Psyche's very different, of course. Who knows how her past experiences will surface, or when? It would be tougher but a lot quicker if she would come back to The Transition with me for some sessions. But it's almost too late and I expect Gerry will influence her away from it. Their sad little plot! "Oh I was just passing, thought I'd just drop in." Will Gerry look out for her? Dad won't, not really, not any more. He can't.

I must concentrate on my further evolution. It will proceed, they won't be able to stop it. I shall go with you and the others, to Mexico, or wherever they are going. It is inevitable.

Chapter Seven

Psyche After All

I t was still quite early as we sat opposite each other at the table and talked quietly. Psyche hadn't slept much. She thanked me again.

"There was no one else she could turn to."

I wanted to give The Transition a rest and talk about her so I asked her about her singing.

Her course at the Royal College of Music was going well, she told me, but she didn't feel at home there. She didn't feel she belonged.

"Where have you belonged, where do you belong? Tony clearly feels he belongs in The Transition now, a new home for him. Where and how do any of us belong? "

An unexpected smile softened her tired and anxious face.

"That's just the sort of thing Terry asks people."

"Oh, sod that then, let's not get too existential. How's the course going, I mean, what are you singing? Any jazz?"

"The course is entirely square, though some of us try to sing a little jazz in our own time. There's a boy who plays a bit of jazz piano."

"Aha!" I said, looking to tease her. "A pianist, a jazzman, and a boy. H'mmmm...

"Oh come on, Gerry. You know about me and boys. Or girls, in case you are about to ask."

"Do you have...do you feel...any passion, then?"

I was out of my depth, not used to talking to a girl like this. She looked at me for a long couple of seconds, then nodded slowly, twice. "Oh yes," and didn't take her eyes off me. I was feeling confused and a little overwhelmed. She smiled again. "Shall we stick to the music, for now?"

She seemed much older than I was, although there were only three years between us. I liked the sound of "for now," though I knew that was a risky thing for me to speculate about.

She was singing in their student production of Mozart's "Così fan Tutte," the part of Dorabella.

"I used to think I was a contralto at school and with my private tutor. But at the College, they've opened out my voice, it's developing so much now. They think I'm a plausible mezzo-soprano, suited to classical and baroque music, possibly not a coloratura soprano for the big nineteenth-century romantics."

I just about knew what she was talking about. "Well, that sounds just fab, Psyche. I much prefer the eighteenth century to those sentimental Italians. Puccini was so shameless really, don't you think?"

This was threadbare stuff, and she looked down, trying to hide a smile.

"So...can I hear you sing?" I asked, out of desperation as well as genuine interest.

"I'd really like that. Come to "Così," it's our end of year show in a month or so."

We fell silent for a moment, just watching each other.

"How good to talk like this. I know you're Tony's best friend, but I really feel now that you and I can be real friends too."

I beamed. "Friends it is, Psyche."

Her pyjama top was low-cut. I wasn't sure I trusted myself. I was still powerfully drawn to her. Good job she didn't like the idea of sex with boys. Good job Bethan did. Too neat a summing up but it would have to do for now.

She stood up. "I'll throw some clothes on and knock up some breakfast. Tony'll be surfacing soon, he has to go to work."

Of course. If he wasn't a student any longer, what did he do, except let the bloody Transition drive him round the bend?

"What work?"

"George bought him a record shop and he runs it. It's pretty cool actually, we could go round there and spy on him later." She disappeared into her room.

I realised how close she felt to her brother and remembered how coldly angry Tony had got with me when I was unkind about her back in the autumn. And I felt, from nowhere, an unpleasant lurch, a low empty feeling, nothing to do with me. It was about Psyche and Tony but I had no idea what it meant or where it came from.

The standard Palmera coffee and croissants eased me back into a more normal frame of mind. Perhaps it was Tony's Beyond speaking to me, I thought dismissively. Tony sat with us for his breakfast. He didn't say much but he looked less strained than the previous evening.

"I'm pleased to see you two talking like friends," he said. He looked directly and unblinkingly at both of us in turn, almost formally. Psyche told him that we were going to drop in on his shop and be a nuisance.

"We'll ask for rare imports and sneer at how you categorise your records."

He managed a smile. "Great, I could always throw you out. See you later then."

After he'd gone, I told Psyche I thought her brother had changed, even down to how he looked at people.

"Oh, that's The Transition stare," she said. "They get people staring at each other just a yard apart for ages. It feels very strange. And they say honest things to you, about you, right in your face, which can be quite unpleasant, and – "

"Why? I mean, what on earth for?"

"It's because what they are saying to you is what they really think, not through the usual social filters. But they haven't met you before, or at least they don't know much about you, so it's not that horrid. And it sort of...teaches you...how to be direct. And you get used to using that direct stare when you're talking to people."

I realised I was staring at her.

"Psyche, they've not got hold of you too, have they?"

She looked down and answered thoughtfully.

"No. But nearly, I think. It's quite useful if you don't really know who you are." She looked back at me, smiled, and shrugged.

"Come on, let's go and buy one of his records, cheer him up."

I walked along beside her from the Tube to the shop, just off the Charing Cross Road, which I thought was dangerously close to Dobell's, the best jazz record shop in town. Psyche seemed unusually carefree, light-hearted even. I was less cheerful, because I was hoping she wasn't relying on me to change Tony's mind. It seemed likely to me that he had decided to go with The Transition wherever they went, whatever the cost to her and to his father.

To try and cheer myself up, I started to tell Psyche a little bit about my life in Liverpool. Certainly time, I felt, to tell her about Bethan so she didn't think I was going to try anything on her. Because I wasn't, was I? I asked myself. An unanswerable question.

"Bethan's just great, quite different from my London life."

Psyche looked at me a little sideways. "You mean quite different from me?"

Oh dear. I hadn't intended to set up comparisons.

"Well, yes," I said, "but also different from George and Tony and the flat and The Elephant and the parties round here. She's not really a city lass. She's a lovely, steady, bright girl from North Wales."

And, I thought, you wouldn't go out with me and she will, and it's great.

Psyche actually seemed pleased to hear about Bethan. I guessed she thought it meant I wouldn't try to take matters any further with her.

I considered this as we walked along. Bethan's home life was a long way from the aspirations of my ex-school friends and from the worldliness of George's flat. Although, in some ways, Psyche wasn't really all that worldly. But then neither was Tony, with his Transition stuff.

I was confusing myself and I was pleased when Psyche said, "Well you can stop being so silent and thoughtful, because here's Tony's shop."

He was cautiously pleased to see us and we tried to make a nuisance of ourselves until a customer came in. Tony seemed remarkably uninterested in making a sale. If a potential customer asked him to play a little of something he didn't like, they got a brief version of The Stare. After an unfortunate incident concerning Ken Dodd's latest single, he put on Dylan's "Bringing It All Back Home" and turned it up.

"What do you think?"

"Completely brilliant," I said.

"He can't sing, but he's interesting," said Psyche the singer.

He turned it off abruptly, walked to the door, turned the Open/Closed sign round and said "Come on, let's have lunch."

In a café nearby, we had a pleasant, lively chat. I watched Tony's reactions and how he spoke. He was still remote, still behind a glass screen. We talked about Psyche's course, about "Così," about my cricket, about his shop, which didn't seem greatly to engage him. I wondered, not for the first time, where George's money came from. We all avoided discussing The Transition and the Mexico trip. And I told them more about my Liverpool life.

Tony turned to me. "Are you sleeping with Bethan, then?"

Psyche immediately jumped in. "Tony, that's none of our business."

There was a pause. I was surprised at how unembarrassed I felt, though I blushed.

"Yes, since you ask. Would you like some further details?"

Tony said "Absolutely not. Poor girl!"

We all laughed.

We left Tony at his shop. Psyche's behaviour puzzled me. Maybe I expected people to run in straight lines, to be reasonably consistent and understandable, at least most of the time. It wasn't just that she was changeable; it was that, somehow, the changes didn't always seem to fit one person. And she had said that she didn't really know who she was. More confusion.

"What are you looking studious about now, Gerry?" Expecting a playful face, I looked up. She was watching me intently, seriously.

"You know, Psyche, sometimes I just can't see into your heart, can't read you. I mean, I never saw the boy problem thing coming, and – "

"Well you had only known me a couple of days."

"True. But then I never saw Martin coming either. And yet other times you are so clear, like a pool of water. It's as though your eyes really are the windows of your soul, as the poet said."

"Stop it, Gerry, or I'll fall in love with you...more than I am already, of course," she said, trying to be light-hearted. But it didn't really sound light-hearted at all.

I stopped dead on the pavement and stared at her. I was totally confused, even a little irritated. After everything that hadn't happened between us.

"Do you realise what you're saying?"

She stared back, then dropped her gaze. "I'm sorry about Martin. I was a bit...desperate. I didn't know...I don't know...""

She was getting upset. I took both her hands, and started to speak. "It's okay, Psyche, really, it's none – "

She looked up quickly, pulled me towards her, and kissed me gently on the lips, with her hand on the back of my neck. I responded gently. She held me for a few seconds, then let me go, backed away a little holding both my hands and looked at me almost appraisingly. Then she raised her eyebrows and shrugged, with a helpless little smile. I let one hand go and held the other as we walked on. Like sweethearts, like lovers. Like an enigma.

Before we reached the flat, Psyche let go of my hand.

"I don't know what to do with you," she said, looking at the pavement.

I immediately thought of something she could do with me, but I sat on my inner schoolboy, told him to shut up, and waited. With some girls, I already knew, you could be cheerfully crude or direct, but there was something about Psyche that stifled any lurking coarseness.

We went into the flat, sat down, put on some music, had a cup of tea. I won't say we talked about the weather, but we were not far off it. I waited and watched her.

"Why are you staring at me?"

"I'm sorry. You are a beautiful mystery. Of course I want to stare at you."

"You say the nicest things."

"Nothing but the truth, so help me God."

She started to well up. I took her hand again.

"Why did you kiss me?"

"Because I wanted to. Because you are you. The sort of person who would hitch down from Liverpool in response to a phone call from a neurotic girl."

I found myself rubbing the back of her hand gently with my thumb, almost massaging each knuckle.

"What's with the neurotic? You've every reason to be worried about Tony. You know more about this bloody Transition thing than I do and I'm worried enough about him."

The front door swung open and Tony came in. He couldn't have heard what we were saying from outside, yet he said "You don't have to worry about me. I have a clearer idea than ever before of who I am and where I'm going."

I had always thought the expression "his jaw dropped" was a lame cliché but that's exactly what happened to me.

Psyche jumped in. "I know, Gerry. He's done that sort of thing before. I said it was a coincidence, he says there is no such thing as a coincidence, the Beyond tells them so, and Jung too."

Thinking about it afterwards, I decided against paranormal communication or the collective unconscious. After all, I was there because Tony's sister and his father were very worried about him, he knew that. But there was something about the way he had followed on exactly from what I had been saying that disconcerted me, along with his calm confidence that he would be right. My unexamined reliance on rational thought and discourse had wobbled, even though I wasn't able to admit it yet. He must have seen it in my face.

"Ha! So Rational Man meets The Inexplicable," said Tony, and helped himself to tea.

"Put his hand down, Psyche, you don't know where it's been." She blushed and I laughed, relieved to see my friend Tony emerging again for a moment from behind the glass screen.

"So I'm going away."

He held his hand up to prevent interruption.

"And what I want to know is, do you, Gerald, and you, Psyche, promise to take care of each other through thick and thin, in sickness and in health and all that? If so, I pronounce you true friend and true friend."

He turned his hand into a priest's gesture of blessing.

"I do, unholy father," I said.

Psyche didn't turn her gaze away from my face.

"I do, and I think you mean, until you return?"

"Until I return new-made, to bring you blessings from afar. But actually, for as long as you both want to be friends."

I loved them both so much at that moment, I couldn't speak. I got up and wandered over to the hi-fi, flipping through the LPs. Oscar Peterson's relentless, flawless swing, not too loud, just right. "Things Ain't What They Used To Be." I wanted to say, "They ain't, my dears, too true they ain't. Come back to us, Tony, and be again what you used to be." But there was no point in arguing with him, at least not about The Transition itself. We three talked about it all, without George, for the first time.

"You seemed puzzled by my deliberately un-business-like approach to the shop. How can I be diverted into caring about a bloody record shop? I really can't. It was kind of Dad but it's a dead end and I'm not going to get stuck in it."

"Okay, but that doesn't mean you have to piss off to Mexico, does it?"

"Yes, it does, Psyche. Can't you see the difference in me? I'm made powerful in my very being after a session with Terry and after a group meditation. I have go with them. I wish so much that you two would come to Mexico with us. Talking to you now, Gerry, it's like watching someone speak clearly but distantly."

I felt sad at this, and scared. Where will this end? It showed in my face and Tony saw it.

"Look, I can't lose you, but I can't stay with you. I have to go. I have to travel with The Transition. No turning back. I'm sorry. Truly I am."

Psyche and I were both looking glum. He tried to offer us something but it didn't amount anything.

"Maybe when I am fully realised and re-named I can speak to you so you truly understand. Maybe."

I understood quite enough of the whole wretched business. I wanted to de-rail it, not understand any more of it. In my pain, all I could think of was something practical.

"Couldn't you just wait a bit, Tony? What seems to trouble George is that that you're under 21. He feels completely responsible for your well-being. And actually, he is. Just wait a bit until you see how The Transition group develops."

Hopeless.

"It will develop, with me. We function as one, for some of the time, at least. We're further on than you can realise, from the outside. In the Caribbean, we will be one all the time. That's the point."

Psyche, surprisingly tough: "And what will you do if George makes you a ward of court?"

Tony didn't know what that meant and as she explained it to him, his face went hard. There was a painful silence.

"Would he really do that?"

"He might. He probably thinks he's saving your sanity, your well-being."

"I care about him, I respect his sense of responsibility towards me but if he does that, he will drive me further away, sooner."

Psyche looked desolate but she persisted.

"You would be breaking the law if you disobeyed the court, as a ward."

"First, they'd have to catch me. How long does it take? The legal stuff, I mean."

I could see that if we weren't careful, we'd be helping him draw up his escape plan. "We're not lawyers, Tony."

"Well, you obviously know more about the fucking law than I do." He was starting to sound tetchy.

"I guess it would vary from case to case. And, of course, he may not do any such thing. Just a possibility."

"Good old Gerry," he said, "the classic Libra, looking for the middle way, calming the waters. If they can be calmed."

I shrugged.

'But I don't think they can be. I'm very sorry about that, very sorry indeed. I think it must be in the stars."

"The stars ..." said Psyche, with the nearest she could manage to a sneer.

But I knew something that she probably didn't. At school, Tony had got into astrology, studied it and taken it seriously. He maintained a superficially sceptical attitude in conversation but he enjoyed talking to someone he hardly knew and then telling them their star sign. He was nearly always right, dammit.

All he said was "There are more things in heaven and earth, Horatio, than are dreamt of in your philosophy."

"You bin readin' them books again, boy Tony?"

He looked at me and smiled. It was a fond smile, but he still had that remote quality to him.

"If your bard was around today, he'd be in The Transition with us. He'd be one of the Elect."

"The what?"

He sighed. "One of our prefects, if you like."

"So it's quite hierarchical, then?"

"No more than it needs to be."

"Are you one of the elect?"

"Time will tell."

This was like bowling at one of those opening batsmen who just blocks and blocks. I gave in.

"Okay. What shall we three do this evening, in thunder lightning and in rain?"

"When indeed shall we three meet again," said Psyche mournfully.

What we did was go to an Italian restaurant, thence to The Elephant and get drunk. It was a relief to talk nonsense loudly and laugh foolishly at foolish things. A big relief for all of us and for me to see more of my friend and less of a Transition product. Looking back on it, it was like a farewell party for the young man we loved.

All three of us got up late, and lounged around the flat for a few hours. I felt like a fully enrolled member of the Palmera Floating World, and an anxiety steadily grew within me. I pretended to read a newspaper and tried to think clearly. How was I going to move back into my Liverpool life with Bethan, after all this intensity? George's beautiful daughter might want me but might just need a friend. And

Liverpool, Bethan my lover, my friends. Maybe I could live in and out of both worlds? Quite a stretch. I gave up.

No sign of George. Tony told me he often stayed away, sometimes for a day or two and his work sometimes takes him abroad.

"What is his work, Tony, I realise I've never asked him."

"Just as well. He wouldn't answer, or rather, he would answer without actually saying anything much. He's in business, export-import, and it's doing well."

"Okay, none of my business anyway." What a puzzling family. "I must head back up north soon."

Tony had one last try. A long look. I waited.

"Chuck it Gerry. They can't teach you much more, at least, not the important things about yourself and the world. Come and explore the world and yourself with me."

"If I come, you think maybe Psyche will too? Is that it?"

"I want you to come so you can discover who you really are. If Psyche came too, that would be wonderful."

Wouldn't it, I thought. And I carried on thinking.

No. It was clear to me that The Transition wasn't my scene. In fact I was scared by it and I didn't like the idea that Tony might have thought of using me to get Psyche onside. I couldn't say that to him.

"Tony. Thank you for – "

"Look, fuck being polite. Just – "

"No, Tony. I value my studies, my friends up there..."

"And Bethan?"

"And Bethan, yes. But that doesn't mean I don't value you, my friend, and Psyche."

I looked up, and he was watching me. "Take care of her, Gerry, whatever happens between you."

"Tony, I will. What are you doing now?"

"I've got a session with Terry and The Elect. So this is goodbye for now, I'll see you when I get back."

"Are you off soon?" I suddenly felt a bit panicky. I knew I couldn't argue or stall him any longer.

"Well now, that would be telling." He grinned unexpectedly. "Might depend on the lawyers."

We only shook hands but he held on to mine longer than usual.

"Please take care of yourself," was all I said.

After he'd gone, Psyche came in and announced she was going to buy me a rail ticket by way of saying thanks. "No need," I muttered, though I was pleased at the gesture. Funds were a bit tight, as usual, and it was a long and tedious hitch, in the days before motorways were completed and linked up.

"In fact," she said, "I'd like to come with you as far as Euston, so we can talk and...be together," she said, almost shyly. Then, as if she had just made up her mind, she came close to me

"But first..."

She took my hand and led me into her bedroom. My pulse-rate zoomed. Closing the door behind me, she pressed me back against it and kissed me hard and long. I was astonished, a bit scared, and didn't really know what to do. Apart from respond. Abruptly, she took my hand and shoved it down the front of her jeans. I realised she hadn't done them up, the zip slid down and my hand was inside her knickers.

"This is all," she panted, "not the full treatment. Come on, then."

"Sure," I panted back at her.

She clutched at me, pushed her face into my neck, thrust herself into my hand, grunted and gasped, until she had finished.

We sat on her bed. She told me she loved me, but she was not going to interfere with my relationship with Bethan. She expected nothing in return, just to see me sometimes, especially while Tony was away. And she thanked me for what I had just done.

"I'm so sorry I can't do the whole performance with you," looking down at the floor. "That must have been...frustrating for you."

"It's okay, really, I loved it. Anyway, I, er...well, I might need a change of clothing before we go." She looked up at me and smiled.

"I'll try and explain it to you one day. I feel I can talk to you about anything."

"It's great you feel that. Because you can. We are soul-mates, not just friends." I didn't really know what I was saying but I didn't want this closeness to end.

"I'm going to splash out on a taxi," she said. I thought it might be so we could talk, but she didn't say much all the way to Euston. She just leaned against me and held my hand. She was calm and a little withdrawn. After she bought my ticket at the station, she hugged me and wouldn't let go for a while, then a quick kiss, and she was gone.

I felt overwhelmed, perplexed and a little desolate on the train, not knowing when I'd be aboard the Floating World again and wondering at how much that mattered. How could I weigh it against my Liverpool life? I gave up and went to sleep.

"So how's Tony?" demanded Bethan next day. "Still mind-boggled?" She'd early on decided that The Transition was a bundle of nonsense and in many ways she was right, of course she was.

"More to the point, how's his sister?" I'd noticed she didn't want to say Psyche's name. She looked hard at me, and kept looking.

"Did you sleep with her?"

"No," I said truthfully.

She kept looking.

"No, I did not sleep with her, but I might sleep with you this evening if we get half a chance."

"You should be so lucky," Bethan answered.

"Indeed so I would, cariad."

"Oh, it's the Welsh coming out now, is it, indeed to goodness, look you? When he wants a proper good screw?"

And as we went on teasing, the tension drained away and something familiar and very valuable came back, bit by bit, into my heart.

How can an old man recreate the passions and perplexities of youth? There I was, back with Bethan, my friends, my cricket. Here I am now, looking back down the pathways and back-alleys I never took. One thing I remember clearly: I couldn't decide, in any open and rational way, how to balance my relationship with Bethan against my sort-of relationship with Psyche. Fate, or whatever, would take its course, I decided, as I walked out to open the batting one chilly morning in May. I loved the smell of the mown grass, of the linseed oil I'd rubbed into my new bat. Those are still powerfully nostalgic smells for me even now. Back then, the pads strapped to my legs made me feel significant. I was opening batsman and I felt surprisingly calm. I'd heard that Keele had a good team for a pint-sized new university. Well, I'd stick around for as long as I could, see if I could wear down the bowling a bit.

I hardly saw the first ball. Next ball went past my outside edge. The wicket keeper sucked his teeth and muttered something. H'mm, this man is really pretty quick, I thought. The slip fielders moved in and the third ball, a yorker, came at my feet. I rammed my bat down just in time, the force of the ball turned the bat slightly in my grasp and the ball shot away for a boundary. The bowler stood with his hand on his hips and glared at me. "Like they do," I thought. And with no warning, the feeling of Psyche's body wet under my hand came to me just for a moment. I looked back at the bowler blankly, elsewhere for a moment.

I came forward to the next ball and drove it hard back towards the bowler, who dived for it and missed. Another boundary. My team-mates were clapping and cheering me on. "It's Psyche who came back to me out of the blue," I thought, "not Bethan." I wondered if that meant anything. And I wondered why I was thinking about any girl, when what I needed to do was to concentrate on the bowling. So I did, and settled down for a few overs of my usual cautious job of blocking, taking care, respecting the bowling, chipping a single or two, building an innings.

That evening in the pub, my team-mates were pulling my leg as usual. "Well, Boycott, we had a flash of Bradman in the first over, so what happened there? Rush of blood to the head?"

I didn't know what had happened. It wasn't my style and when I tried another defiant drive some 30 runs later, I heard the horrible sound of a disintegrating wicket behind me. I began the long trudge back to the pavilion.

Chapter Eight

Lawyers and Exits

A fter the weekend of my unexpected intimacies with Psyche, the weekend of saying goodbye to Tony, I heard nothing from him or his sister and my Liverpool life just rolled forward towards the end of the summer term.

Then he was in the newspapers. George had done exactly what he said he'd do: he'd moved to have Tony made a ward of court. Tony and Johnny Walker got a solicitor who found some legal loophole in the proceedings and while all that was being worked through, The Transition caravan simply left with Tony and Johnny. They flew out to the Caribbean via Mexico.

There was a short TV newsreel moment of a journalist trying to interview Tony outside the flat; the journalist got nowhere. There was a shadowy figure in the open doorway, which I was pretty sure was Psyche. I felt a warm flush and turned away from the TV.

"So what's going to happen to your friend now?" asked Bethan.

"I wish I knew."

"You look upset."

"He's one of my best friends. No. He's my very best friend. I don't know what's going to happen to him. Of course I'm bloody well upset."

"You're getting overwrought, Gerry." Long pause, face turned up to mine, a hard look. "He's not...you weren't...well, you know...a queer, a poof?"

Bethan was not narrow-minded or what we would now call homophobic. It was just how people spoke then. Straight people, at least.

"No, nothing like that." It was too difficult to try to recreate for her the strange world of a boy's boarding school and the sort of friendships it generated that had a particular intensity even when they weren't gay.

"Nothing like that."

She did her best to cheer me up but alongside my worries about Tony, there was the realisation that a blurred TV picture of someone, who might or might not be Psyche, was enough to disturb me. I wasn't very good company for a day or two and, quite understandably, Bethan got fed up with it all. I was a bit lost.

So was Tony, though he never would have accepted the idea. The journey had started off with some satisfying cloak-and-dagger stuff. Journalists and George turned up at Heathrow at the pre-arranged time for The Transition flight but they'd left the previous day. Eventually, everyone knew they were in Honduras but we didn't know their specific location until they were settled.

After he got back, Tony told me his story, bit by bit, in sessions in The Transition House or in a quiet corner at The Elephant. I still have Tony's increasingly fragmentary diary from this time.

"Mexico City en route was a gas...perhaps a bit too much of a gas really, I wanted to get on with Transition. A lot of sessions later, it became clear from the Beyond that we should head down to the north coast of Honduras."

He was feeling some ambivalence by then. It was increasingly clear to him that he was not one of the Elect, the inner circle round Terry. He was one of the youngest of the expedition. The young ones tended to form up as a group but Tony had an intense drive about him that jarred with their excitable chatter. He felt left a little to one side.

"To make matters worse, we were getting low on cash. The diet got steadily worse. The heat was flattening. But that was okay, I reckoned. We needed to be tested, thrown together. I felt that some of us might not make it. Actually, I rather hoped some of them wouldn't."

"What about the hierarchy, your leader and the Elect?"

"Terry kept apart even more than in London. I felt his power growing. He created our sense of direction. When he appeared, we were all really pleased to see him and we wanted his attention. He was so quick to take on what we had just said. He could turn it in his hands so it reflected the light differently, so it was part of what was unfolding, not just a random comment. But then, he was always able to do that."

"And that's how he maintained his power, his control over you."

"Gerry, shut up. You don't understand, couldn't...you weren't there..."

"I never will understand, and I'm happy with that."

Tony sighed. That was the end of that session.

Next time we talked, he told me that he hadn't spent much time with Johnny. It seemed like just a chance they were at the same school and hung out in London. Johnny was entrusted by the Elect to deflect members if they wanted to see Terry, or if they asked too many questions.

"He pissed me off sometimes."

It seems The Beyond didn't like the fishing village where they first arrived and they waited for some direction. Abruptly, Terry and some of the Elect left, telling the rest to sit tight until they were called for. They lounged around trying not to get any more sunburned or mosquito-bitten, feeling hungry and a bit deserted.

"And yet you didn't want to chuck it and come home?"

"Absolutely not. It was all huge, new, I wasn't the Beige creature I'd been in London." He paused, searching, remembering.

"I did miss you, Gerry, and Psyche. And Dad, I suppose. But I don't think you could've hacked this."

"Not as tough as Tony the Psychic Warrior, then…"

My irritation with the whole wretched business was making me unkind.

"Sorry, Tony."

"You couldn't have stood it only because you didn't have the core of belief and trust in The Transition. That would've made it impossible for you."

Eventually they were all summoned by the senior members and told to walk on along the shore to a special place chosen for them, destined for them. It was a ruined, roofless mansion, with a few small huts inside dilapidated stone walls. Tony said they were directed there by The Beyond. So they all set to, clearing the place up, repairing the huts.

"We were still starving and burnt to buggery but I felt we really were on track now. This was our new home, a Transition base."

With the new home came a new development: if Terry decided one of them had transgressed they were invited to flagellate themselves.

"I was scared of it, but was actually a bit of a high."

"What?" This story was moving way beyond my sense of what was real. It was turning into a fable of pointless suffering and cruelly distorted idealism.

'You did what?"

"Nothing like those creepy sadists at Dallinghoo, Gerry. It was a reality-flash, a move outside of myself. I bellowed and yelled while I was doing it. That helped. And then I went and sat in the shade to recover.

"Tony, you were spinning out of our orbit. Psyche and I could do nothing. Why didn't you at least write letters and tell us what was going on?"

"Well actually, I tried...started. One of the Elect suggested I stop writing letters. Said having private thoughts and conversations with the Beige was taking me away from higher group consciousness, the evolving Transition. Separated me from the group. And you know, I could see his point."

I couldn't; it seemed like a creepy intervention into his private self. At this point, we were sat in a café on Kensington High Street, so far, in every way, from what he was describing. I watched the rain running down the window, people hurrying past in coats, under umbrellas.

Tony could see I was not attending to him.

"Look, if you're tired or..."

"No, sorry. Go on. I want to try and understand."

"Well, we had arrived in Mexico each of us with a little bundle of private stuff. Gradually, we gave up on that and pretty much everything was shared. Our middle-class habits were evolving out of us. Terry said we needed to be as One, to live in harmony with the One. It was taking struggle and effort and hardship, all of which were good signs. If it was easy, why would we bother?"

"Why not tell the Elect to get stuffed? Your letters were none of their business, surely."

Tony looked at me, shaking his head.

"See, that just shows how little you really get of it all. I got tired of some of the Elect and some of us ordinary Transitioners were silly, distracting me from the Path. But what Terry said...his words opened on out, led me and the rest of us on. I just wish he had spent more time with us. But perhaps that's why, when we did see him, what he said really resounded. It was the power of his inner self, his vision, his insight and dedication that led us."

"Okay. Tell me more."

He did, over the next few days.

I understand more fully now how the centripetal power developed. Terry was a very skilful moulder of people's spirits, their psyches. Especially people in their late teens and early twenties. He took the smallest statement or thought and turned it around to link the person's sense of identity with the onward path he was marking out for them. He made the group identity paramount and their individual psyches eroded gradually away. And that was how they put up with so much.

They had to go for a walk in the woods when they needed a shit. They washed with sand and salt water. They were sore with sunburn and stiff with salt. Most of them were losing weight. Some of the girls stopped menstruating. In discussion, they agreed that sex mattered very little to them. It seemed part of a trivial and sex-obsessed world to which they used to belong. Now, they were creating a new world around themselves. They all looked terrible. Some of the girls wore very little. In London, that would have encouraged competition amongst the blokes and possibly some sexual relationships, but not any more.

When Terry emerged to call the group together, he looked neat and comparatively well groomed. This the group members generally accepted. They were used to being led from above now. It seemed right that Terry was cared for so he could save his energies to share with them the way ahead and the part each of them had to play in it.

Tony's story moved slowly towards a huge, dangerous climax. Small events are increasingly interpreted as significant signs that they are all chosen agents of The Beyond, connected to infinite power. Larger events, such as the arrival of some money from a worried parent or friend, are given almost cosmic significance. The power of the group feeling, the unchallenged dominance of Terry, grows rapidly. Then one day, a heavy, humid day, someone says:

"Look at the sea. No, I mean, really, look at it."

It had a leaden, sullen, oily look, and in place of the regular gentle surf, there was a rolling swell, getting steadily stronger. A powerful wind gusted fitfully, the coconut palms began to sway – and the army arrived.

The soldiers tell them to get out, they will evacuate them and take them to an inland town. There's a hurricane coming. The young people stand around not knowing what to do. One of the soldiers starts to shout: "Huracan! Cycloney! Vamos! Is big cylconey!"

Someone says "Oh shit. I'm scared."

"What do we do?" Someone starts to cry.

Then Terry appears, neat and tidy, pressed shorts, clean shirt. He listens to the soldier, and asks him to wait

"Diez minutos, por favor, Señor." The soldier goes back to the van and leans against it, shaking his head. Terry disappears with the Elect. They sit around in silence. "Well?" he says eventually. "I'm getting...flight, safety," says the most cautious one. Turning to stare round the group, Johnny Walker says, "Stay. We have been chosen to stay. We must." Terry looks at him for a full, silent minute. "We stay," he says. One of the Elect says that it's a huge opportunity to strengthen the group, and disappears back into his room.

He walks outside and speaks to them all.

"If anyone wants to go, just leave in the van with the soldiers.

You will not be criticised or blamed, and we will meet up with you again in good time. But hurry."

Three people dart off and collect their pathetic little bundles. Terry walks, slow and calm, up to the senior soldier, who stares at him as he approaches. "These go," he says, as the three run up behind him. "The rest stay. Thank you for coming to us. Muchas gracias. Vaya con Dios." He keeps staring at him. Shakes his head in bemusement, lets the three into the van, climbs in next to the driver and leans out of the window. "I pray you safe," he says and the van roars off.

There is an unworldly sense of freedom and glee amongst those who stay. One of them says "Well, that has sorted the sheep from the goats. The true Transitionists have stayed."

Terry turns his stare on her.

"That is wrong. There is one Transition." The girl looks down and blushes. But they are too busy to worry about who is true to The Transition or not. For the next few hours they do their best to make some shelter out of a couple of doors and other bits of discarded timber. All they can do is prop them up against one of the huge walls. The wind rises steadily until you have to yell in someone's ear to be heard above the roaring hissing wind and sea. Terry and the Elect retreat to their little four-roomed stone hut. The rest huddle against the lee side of one of the stone walls, crouching under the timbers they have put up.

The rain arrives abruptly. It is beyond British experience, comparison or concept. It is as though a waterfall were crashing down on them, smashing into their flimsy shelter as though it were not there. They start to shiver as they crouch, their thin tropical summer clothing wet through in moments. Someone chants something. Someone else laughs hysterically.

"A freshwater shower at last," he yells.

Time loses coherence. Have they been soaked and battered for ten minutes or three hours? Then someone gets up to a crouch and points to what he thinks will be a slightly more sheltered place. They look at each other and one by one get up and stagger after him, through the howling turmoil, to the lee side of a roofless stone hut. They slump, lean, sit, hold each other in a state of desperate exaltation. Some look resentfully at the neat stone building where the Inner Circle are. Some of them are so exhausted by tension and effort, they actually doze. The rain eases. Then In a moment, everyone is wide awake.

"What's that?"

"Earthquake?"

A voice cries out in fear, as a rolling, rumbling thunder makes the ground tremble underneath them. People throw themselves flat, clutch each other. Tony looks round the end of the hut. And says "Fuck me!"

A great wall had completely collapsed and huge blocks of stone had crashed down exactly where they had all been sheltering. They ran through the storm, whooping and cheering, across to the Elect hut and kicked the door open, jabbering and yelling at them. "Sit DOWN" said Terry, who almost never raised his voice. They told him what had happened. He smiled, nodded a couple of times and told them to sleep where they could. Which they did.

Chapter Nine

George's Question

It must have been about the time that The Transition arrived in Honduras that I was called down again to the phone in the hall. I half expected, and certainly hoped, that it would be Psyche's voice in my ear. I was startled to hear George.

"Gerry, George here." He sounded as calm as ever. "I don't want to be a nuisance."

"I think that's pretty unlikely, George," I replied, trying to be light-hearted, but in fact I was anxious about whatever it was he wanted to say.

"Are you playing cricket this weekend? If not, could you come down to the flat?"

I reassured him that there was no match and I could probably skip a training session without getting dropped.

"I've got a few thoughts I'd like to run past you...about Tony. I'll see you Friday evening. Okay?"

"Of course. I'll be there, George, and ..."

"You'll be staying here, of course, and I'll reimburse the train fare, and so on." He had taken control, as he so often had done with me, and it was done effortlessly. I didn't try to protest too much.

I hadn't been to the flat for over a month. It occurred to me on the London train that I hadn't really been looking after Psyche, as I'd promised her brother I would. I'd sent her a postcard, in the aftermath of Tony's departure, which simply said "You okay?" So cool. She had rung me back and we had a brief inhibited little chat. I hated talking in the hallway with people wandering past.

I remembered noting that she never called her father "Dad," as Tony did. And George was away a lot. Perhaps it was as simple as that: a remoteness in her relationship with George, worries about Tony, and the pressures of a high-level training in singing and performing. But I had promised Tony I would look after her. Still, Psyche was a 22-year old talented young woman living in a lovely flat with her wealthy father. How much did she really need looking after? And here I was, risking my relationship with Bethan. It all went round and round. I gave up and read my book all the way to Euston.

After I rang the bell, it took a good few moments before I heard George unlocking and opening the door. He stood aside to let me in. I looked quickly round the room. George smiled. "She's out, rehearsing. You'll have to put up with me. Thank you for giving us the time, it's good to see you."

He disappeared into the kitchen and emerged with drinks and snacks. He had no domestic help, so he must have prepared them himself. We sat at the table and he looked at me for what seemed an awkwardly long time. He spoke as calmly as usual.

"You're Tony's closest friend, aren't you?

"Yes, though he went to Mexico City with Johnny, so…"

"That's only because you wouldn't go, which was very sensible of you. And Johnny..." he held hands out and apart, as if to release Johnny from consideration, "is a pleasant enough misguided youth." He put his hands on the table and leaned forwards. "So it's your view that counts."

"Okay ..." I felt hesitant, anxious. "So, George?"

"Because Tony is a minor, I can get him back. The lawyers have sorted themselves out at last."

"Good."

"Yes, but is it, Gerry? I want to ask you if you think it will destroy my relationship with my son if I intervene."

"George..." I felt able, for the first time, not to feel over-awed by him. "That's a huge question and, well...isn't it a big responsibility you are putting on me?"

I got the level, thoughtful gaze. I managed to hold it. I felt, abruptly, that his super-cool manner was irrelevant here. A vulnerable father, of course. Who else could he ask? He's only asking for a view. Get a grip.

"What does Psyche think?"

The gaze didn't move.

"I'm asking you. We will ask her, of course."

"OK. I'll tell you what I think, for what it's worth."

"Gerry, you know this family better than anyone I know. It's worth a lot."

This is for all three of them, I told myself. Focus.

I sat back, had a drink, looked at the floor. Perhaps to go round it all a bit might help.

"How did it go when he said goodbye to you?"

It turned out he didn't. In effect they fled to the airport. George said that the last time he saw Tony, he thought his son seemed excited and resolute.

"How would it work, getting him back?"

"Due process of law via authorities in wherever they are."

"Would he actually come back? Why not just wait until he returns when he wants to?"

For the first and last time ever, George looked a little irritated with me and shifted in his chair before answering.

"Have you met Terry and his Elect? No, I didn't think you had. What do you feel about The Transition?"

"Frankly? I'm scared of it."

"With good reason. They've got him, Gerry. I don't know that we can ever get him out, except by legal process."

I felt dismayed, that cold and empty feeling you get when someone tells you something very bad that you know is true but you really wish it wasn't.

"But...if they all come back, eventually, you can't just keep him away from the rest of them. Can you?"

"I'm hoping that breaking him out of their immediate environment might loosen their hold. Who knows if the rest of them will return? It's the hurricane season in the Caribbean and one is already tearing roofs off. The Transition people are presumably camping out somewhere."

A sense of real dread settled on me. Inadvertently, I muttered "Oh fuck."

George smiled. "Quite. They may of course be fine, they may get evacuated, or what have you. We just need to get him out when we can."

I looked at the table, the floor, anywhere but George's penetrating gaze. I needed to stall.

"Can I just let it all settle a bit?"

"Very good. We'll adjourn. And we'll ask Psyche the same question."

He picked up my bag and led me through to what had been Tony's room. Was it still Tony's room? It was unfamiliar to me and it felt very strange to be there. "George, I might feel...well, it might be better if I did sleep on the sofa, like the old days."

A rare joke: "It's okay, Gerry, I've changed the bed."

It would be rude to insist and it was a very comfortable bedroom, with a phone, and a few excellent photos of London and Londoners on the walls. Little real sense of his presence, belongings all tidied away. Tony was 5,000 miles away, and perhaps his life was in danger.

I rang Bethan from Tony's bedside phone.

"Hello, cariad. I'm installed and discussing Tony's situation with his dad. Just to let you know."

"Oh, thank you for letting me know."

Flat, not very interested. Was she sullen, or simply inhibited because she was at a public phone in her hall?

"I'm sorry to miss another weekend, but..."

"When are you going to stop obsessing about that family and lead your own life?"

Yup. Sullen and detached. She'd not been like that when I left. Maybe she'd had too long to think about it all.

"Friendship matters, and loyalty too, Beth, as I'm sure you'd agree. It's only a couple of days. I just want to help."

"Just make sure you don't bloody well help that Psyche too much. And please don't call me Beth."

And she hung up.

Well, isn't this weekend going nicely, I thought. Then I sat on the self-pity and tried to concentrate on George's question. In my mind I ran through past conversations and situations with Tony, with

George, and with Psyche. Irrelevant queries kept popping up. Why didn't George have domestic help? When did his wife die and what had happened to her? Why was Psyche so much more detached from her father than Tony?

I didn't have any way of dealing with such questions. My thoughts were all over the place. Then Psyche came into the room. I jumped up, flushed, beaming. She hurried over and gave me a long, gentle kiss. I stood back and looked into her face.

"You know why I'm here?"

"I rather hoped it was to see me..."

"I'm sorry. Well, of course. Really. It's so good to see you. But we have a question to discuss, from George. Come on, I've been keeping him waiting."

We talked about the law, about hurricanes and The Transition. We got sad, and angry, and upset – well, Psyche and I did. Psyche couldn't see what there was to discuss.

"He needs to come back, right now."

It wasn't so clear to me. There surely was a risk to the relationship between George and his son.

George sat and listened, occasionally commented, or steered the discussion along. What we didn't talk much about was George as a dad. But I did remind him about the way he'd dealt with those two unpleasant schoolmasters.

"He must have seen that as clear evidence of your...of how much you care about him. Surely he wouldn't turn his back on all that?"

Why couldn't I use the word "love" in this context? Of course George loved his son, or he wouldn't be worried now, wouldn't do what he'd done at Dallinghoo. But somehow the word didn't fit with this thoughtful, restrained, polite, distant figure.

I stood up and wandered over to the window. I looked across to the park, late sun falling across the grass. I thought about next week's cricket match. I'd have to deal with some spin. I was better against pace, really...

Something fell into place. I turned back to George.

"I think you should get him back. Pronto. Psyche?"

"At last. Well of course," she said quietly.

"It might just work. You might be able to actually free him from them. And leaving him there...is just...unethical." I winced inside. What a pronouncement.

"There may be a risk. Are you a risk taker, George?"

Where was all this independence coming from? Must be Psyche's presence.

Unexpectedly, he said, "Yes, I am. Every week. That's business. But this is nearer the heart."

Aha. At last.

He looked down, then at me. Not, I noticed, at his daughter. In fact, they didn't look at each other much. So...what?

"I think you and Psyche are right. It's a risk, but one I must take. He thinks I'm...what do they call us? Beige, that's us. So let's be beige, rational, dull. Let's get him back. I think I have to, even if the outcome is painful for me. It's for Tony."

On impulse, I raised my glass. "Here's to Tony and his safe return."

"Tony," they both echoed.

We should have toasted George and Tony, father and son. What I should have done was to try and answer his original question: if George pulled his son out, would it ruin their relationship?

George took us out for dinner to a well-known French restaurant. He made sure we talked about singing, cricket, jazz, my school, Psyche's school. Tony was hardly mentioned. I got expensively drunk on

Chateauneuf-du-Pape. George and Psyche drank only a little. Late in the meal, I raised a glass and said, a little too loudly, "My second toast this evening: Screw The Transition." Heads at other tables looked round. George smiled a little, Psyche giggled, and we drank to the downfall of the whole damned business.

It was a classic Floating World evening, and despite our anxiety about Tony, I think we all enjoyed it. I certainly did. Psyche wore a Breton-style blue and white top, Her dark waterfall of hair was tied back and she was wearing big silver hoop earrings. Her long legs were in black jeans. I wanted to touch every inch of her.

But I didn't. Not in her brother's bedroom, with her father's room across the corridor. And anyway, the red wine soon put me under.

Chapter Ten

Così

These days, I sometimes think I am not much good at drinking alcohol because of my age, but in fact I don't think I was ever a real boozer. Having been brought up in a pub, I knew a lot about alcohol, that powerful and potentially lethal drug. One thing I re-discovered that morning, in Tony's room, is that a red wine hangover is worse than any other except gin, or mixed drinks.

Psyche woke me with a cup of tea and drew back the curtains. The light skewered my brain and I cowered under the bedclothes. "The curtains," I groaned. She drew them again, came over and sat on the bed. She watched me as I drank a little tea and sank back on the pillow.

"A crapulous morning for you," she said with a smile.

The word was new to me. I let it settle and decided, through my headache, that it was an unpleasantly accurate description of my state. When I opened my eyes a little, she was unbuttoning her pyjama top. I opened my eyes much wider.

"This might help," she said softly, and as I sat up, she reached for my head and held my face between her breasts. I couldn't breathe very easily, but I decided I would prefer to suffocate right there than back off. I reached for her.

"Better not," she said and got up. "George is about." She began buttoning up her top.

"Not too fast, please," I said. "I've not seen them before."

"I'm sure you've seen plenty of others."

"But they are...yours. Incomparable. White doves, lilies of the field ..." The hangover was messing up my feeble store of quotations.

She stood up. "Breakfast?"

George came and sat with us while I tried to eat something and drank plenty of coffee.

"Have you changed your view at all, Gerry? In vino veritas and all that, but also sometimes in vino bombast, and you did have a few last evening."

"Was I too bombastic?"

"No, just lively. But...?"

I tried to concentrate, then I just fell back on my feelings.

"No, I think you can't do much else and..."

"Live with myself?"

I was aware that Psyche was watching me very closely. Those dark eyes.

"Well, yes, I suppose that's it. I mean, only you know your own heart in this, of course."

And now Psyche was gazing at her father, as if she could read his heart. George kept his eyes on me.

"That's true, too. Thank you, Gerry. I might check back with you later in the day, let it settle. Are you staying tonight?"

"Oh do, Gerry." Psyche broke in. "You said you wanted to hear me sing. It's the dress rehearsal of "Così" tonight, the performances are Sunday and Monday. Unless you could..."

"Ah no, I'd best be off tomorrow. But I'd love to come along this evening."

The morning was recovery time, listening to records, walking in the park. Psyche was fairly quiet much of the time. She was worried about Tony and about his relationship with George.

"And with us," she said.

"Us?"

"He'll know we had a hand in George's decision."

"Well, I did, at least. It might be possible for you to remain neutral, since he asked me so directly for my view."

I thought through my conversation with George the previous afternoon, before Psyche came home.

"In fact, although he said he'd involve you in the conversation, he didn't...well, he didn't ask you directly. Why was that?"

"He let me have my say."

"Sure, of course."

She was staring at the ground. I didn't understand what was going on. We sat on a bench and I asked her a question I probably shouldn't have.

"Why do you call him George?"

"That's his name," she said coolly.

"Tony calls him Dad."

"Well, that's his choice."

"Things okay between you?"

She looked at the ground again.

I felt out of order.

"I'm sorry. It's none of my business. It's just that you and your family have rather...captivated me. Mostly you, but not just you. Tony's my best friend. I like and respect George. And I want to understand how it works with you three."

She looked at me distantly, her mind somewhere else.

"Well...it's as you see."

I sighed. "Okay. There's no art to find the mind's construction in the face. I give in."

"Don't give in. I mean, don't give up on me."

Her eyes filled and glistened.

"I don't want to sound like a pop song but, Psyche, I've loved you since I first saw you. That won't change."

Long silence. She took my hand. Very quietly she asked:

"And Bethan?"

My turn for a long pause and a sigh.

"I don't know. It's not just two girls, it's two worlds. Maybe I love you both, in different ways. O God, that's a terrible cliché. Under the heading 'wants to have cake and eat it'. I don't know what to do...I really don't."

Quietly, fiercely: "Don't choose. You needn't choose. Just go on loving me. No one else does, or really has, ever."

When we came into the flat, George was lying on one of the sofas with his feet up. He got up quickly and glided over to us in his silent way. He put a hand on my shoulder and then on Psyche's for a moment.

"All well with you two?"

Did I see a flicker of anxiety underneath his customary calm? He must really be worrying about Tony.

"Fine, George, thanks. In fact, fab."

Psyche wandered off. "How about some tea?" she said over her shoulder. "I have to get there early."

We sat at the table again, the table of investigations and challenges.

"Have your views changed?"

"Let's talk round it and through it. We owe him that," I said pompously.

George looked at me a moment. "We do."

So we did.

"Right," said George after half an hour. "Let's move to vote on the motion before us."

I watched Psyche as I said, "I think it's got to be the law. What do you think, Psyche?'

"You know what I think."

"Carried nem con," I said.

It sounded flippant and lightweight. Maybe I'd had enough of this weight.

George got up. "I'll set the wheels in motion." He disappeared into his room and we heard him talking quietly on the phone.

"On a Saturday afternoon?"

Psyche looked away as she said "He's quite a powerful man you know, Gerry."

And we spoke no more about it.

I knew little of opera, so I read up the plot of "Così Fan Tutte" beforehand. I didn't like it at all, such a silly story. A fatuous and unpleasant intrigue. But Psyche's singing was lovely. Then came what I later learned was the trio "Soave sia il vento."

I understood more fully then why Psyche wanted to enter this extraordinary profession. She could create the purest, most transcendent delight and bring tears to an audience's eyes; she did to mine. Just that morning, I had seen her half-naked. Then she had asked me to love her. And now she could make these sounds for me. Okay, for her audience, including me. And she had to pick her way through this nasty intrigue. Idiotic soldiers, nasty cynical old manipulator.

Afterwards: "What did you think?"

"I hated the plot. Nasty, cynical..."

"Calm down, Gerry, it's only a play."

She looked a little crestfallen. After a pause, during which I winced at my failure to start off with something positive, she said "Did you enjoy my..."

"Your voice is absolutely beautiful and the tunes are just lovely. The farewell to the soldiers, with three of you singing - "

"Soave sia il vento."

"Yes. I've never heard anything more beautiful. Sung by anyone as beautiful."

She leaned her head on my shoulder.

"Thank you, Gerry. That means a lot to me."

"Not that I know anything about opera," I said.

She sat up.

"Don't spoil it. Your ears already know everything that matters."

"Don't know about that, but I do now understand why you work so hard at such a difficult art form, to make the gift of your voice sound out for us all to hear." Perhaps that was an early warning sign of the pomposity that lies in wait for me these days, whenever I want to say something significant. But I meant it. And she smiled.

When we got back to the flat, George had knocked up a light meal for us and sat with us, enjoying Psyche's account of the evening and my enthusiastic responses. His enjoyment was visible in a few smiles, a few nods of the head and finally: "Well done, you talented girl."

He reached over and patted her arm. She looked back at him briefly, then stood up and said, "Let's have a nightcap."

So we did. Psyche went to bed almost at once. I still ached for her, but there was something chastening and calming in the beauty she had created and a gentle goodnight kiss seemed right.

The next morning, because I hadn't had much to drink the previous night, I woke clear-headed and rested. I knew I had to get back to Liverpool and talk things through with Bethan.

Chapter Eleven

Nehemiah

How strange it is that the collapse of a rotten, ancient building in the middle of a storm eventually moved Tony beyond the reach of both Psyche and me. He described the aftermath of the storm for me.

The day after the building collapsed, people woke slowly and late where they had slumped. They lay about, still exhausted and bewildered. They felt a light-headed, washed-out sort of wonder when they stood among the piles of stones and rubble that had once been a towering wall. It had been within minutes of killing them. They looked at each other anew, as survivors, as those chosen to escape. There wasn't much to be said, at first. One or two wept. People shook their heads, grinned at each other almost sheepishly.

They were all very hungry and thirsty and had to set to, fetching and carrying. The wind still buffeted them with fierce gusts as they gathered food. The Elect had withdrawn into their house. As the day wore on with no sign of them, a little gentle gossiping and muttering started up. Then a Senior appeared and told them Terry would be with them in half an hour.

They sat around more or less in a circle and as Terry appeared, neat and orderly as usual, some of them broke into applause. No one knew quite why. He stepped into the centre and sat on one of the stone blocks that could have killed someone. He looked round the whole group, slowly and calmly. The wind still roared in the palms and they could hear the surf thundering on the beach. All he said was: "Well?"

An excited babble broke out. "Another five minutes and..."

"It was Johnny, he led us over there and next thing ..."

"Christ, the power of that storm, I mean ..."

Gradually, they tailed off. Terry began firing questions, leading the answers the way he wanted them to go.

"Why do you think you were spared?"

"It was huge luck."

"Really?" he snapped. Clearly the wrong answer.

"Try again. Think about what has happened since we took off from London."

"Well, we've all meditated together and we have been guided by The Beyond to this place so..."

"Exactly. But why were you spared? Why did The Beyond tell Johnny it was time to move?"

Someone said "Because we were all soaked and freezing."

He got the stare. "You had been wet and cold half an hour before that. You would have been wet cold and dead, ten minutes later. So why exactly then?"

"Because the wall was about to collapse."

"Yes, but you didn't know that, not even Johnny knew that. Why were you spared? Why? Let's concentrate together. You need an answer to that question."

They sat in silence, eyes down or closed. Great gusts of wind buffeted them still. The sun was beating down again, warming bodies that could so easily have been cold and broken.

Someone broke the silence.

"I'm getting something about providence."

"Mmm, yes, spared for a purpose."

Suddenly Johnny spoke, louder and more clearly.

"Yea, though I walk through the Valley of Death, I will fear no evil."

"Yes, yes," people cried out. They looked at Terry, who smiled and suddenly opened his arms wide.

"Johnny, you are Moses. You led your people out of mortal danger, through the water to the other side, the Promised Land. From now on, your name is Moses."

Delight, tears, hugs.

"Why did he lead you to safety? What does the story tell us?"

"So the chosen people could live under God," someone called out almost in a trance.

Gradually, everyone quietened.

Terry spoke into the sound of the wind and the waves, into their rapt attention.

"It is so clear, isn't it? The Beyond has made it plain. We have been chosen to carry our message around the world, so everyone can do what we have just done. And what is it we have done?" he asked, before someone else could.

"Moved forward in our path."

"More," he said. "More."

Johnny stood up and raised both arms in the air.

"Well, Moses?" he asked.

His eyes were closed, his face turned to the sky.

"We have Transitioned. Truly, we have Transitioned."

"YES!" yelled Terry, startling everyone.

More hugs and tears, cries of agreement and affirmation.

From that morning on, Johnny became Moses, one of the Elect. Tony surprised himself by feeling no envy, no jealousy, although Moses was closer to Terry, the centre of their lives. The group identity was never stronger than at that point. In group sessions, other much less significant events were given Biblical levels of significance and more names were changed.

A party, thrown for the friendly, tolerant villagers, proceeded with a mix of carefree happiness and manic glee. Its success was seen by the group as confirmation of a unity with all life in the universe.

"We have broken down the boundaries between our culture and languages and theirs," said one Transitioner. Many of them were convinced they were telepaths and said things like "I'm getting London."

"Me too, that's really strange, isn't it?"

Signs of their Transition As One were everywhere, it seemed. Of all his time with The Transition, Tony enjoyed these days after the storm the most. Nothing much happened. They patched up their living quarters and camping areas as well as they could. Many of them walked back to the village and helped the locals repair their homes.

When the sea had calmed and the fishing boats set out again, their catches were much better than usual, as if the storm was offering up some consolation for the fear and suffering it had brought. At least, that was how Terry presented it to his followers.

Most of the group were still undernourished, suffering from mosquito bites and sunburn, but the general atmosphere seemed more tranquil. Tony was still not part of the Elect, the inner circle, not further up the hierarchy and closer to Terry. So he was pleasantly surprised when in one group meditation, Terry turned to him with the usual stare and paused. Then: "You are often very helpful, Tony.

It's time we clarified your role, and gave you your new name. Let us meditate and see what The Beyond can suggest."

They sat there, eyes closed. "Anyone getting anything?" said someone. "I'm feeling a pull back to London," said Tony.

"Why?" asked Terry sharply.

"I'm not sure. Wait …" he paused for what seemed a long time. "I think we are needed now to spread our word. Things are…getting stranger back there."

"I have your name," Terry cried out." You are now Nehemiah."

As eyes opened, people looked puzzled. Someone asked who Nehemiah was.

"He was in a privileged position close to a king. He is in exile with his people and he hears that back in Jerusalem, people are suffering and their temple is ruined. He speaks to the king, who tells him to return with all he needs to rebuild the Temple and comfort his people."

"But Tony - sorry, Nehemiah - is still here, he's not leaving, is he?"

"Who knows?" answered Terry. "Who knows where next we shall be called?" His rhetoric got more biblical as the sanctification of their mission developed. Tony felt somewhat gratified, though his role was all a little uncertain and it hadn't projected him into the Elect, unlike Johnny Moses.

Unexpectedly, he soon began to move into his new-found prophetic role. Two weeks after collecting his new name, which few of the group used because they found it difficult to pronounce, Tony was sitting in the shade of a hut watching a sweaty little man in a suit walk towards him carrying a briefcase.

"Good afternoon."

Tony continued to look at him.

"I wonder. Are you perhaps Mr Alan Walker?"

Tony pointed to where Johnny was chatting to a couple of the girls.

The Suit seemed mildly disgusted. They all looked to him like half-starved refugees. Maybe they were, but refugees from what?

"So might you be Mr Tony Palmera?"

"I might."

"May I join you? I need to discuss something very important with you."

"Why don't you take your jacket off before you spontaneously combust?"

"Ah yes, good idea."

"You're welcome."

The Suit sat down on a large stone block, remnant of the hurricane's power. He explained that he had papers from London that meant that Tony had to return with him as far as Mexico City, where he would be put on a plane to London. The Suit remained calm and patient while Tony got cross.

"What about my rights as a free UK citizen? I've done nothing criminal."

"Of course not, of course not. But you are under 21 and therefore a minor. The Honduran government states, and I have the papers with me, that your presence here is illegal since you are not accompanied by an adult guardian approved by your father."

"I am accompanied by Terry."

"I am afraid he is most emphatically not approved by your father."

"But I..."

"I'm sorry, Mr Palmera, but you really have no choice in the matter and it would be very unwise to try to ignore the Honduran authorities," almost as if he could read Tony's next thought, "by going on the run."

"I'm sure I could hide away and save you a lot of trouble. Our local villagers are very nice gentle people."

"Let's just say that, in those excellent qualities, they are unlike many of the police. I visit local prisons quite often and believe me, you really don't want to land up in one."

Tony glared at him.

"Who the fuck are you anyway?"

"I'm the nearest British consul to here."

Tony sighed, thought through his situation for a moment and ran out of alternatives to consider.

"How long have I got?"

"No time at all, I'm afraid. Time enough to gather your things and say cheerio to your friends."

"But how..."

"The same taxi I arrived in."

Tony looked at the ground between his feet. After everything he'd been through with this group of people. Back to The Beige. Back to his father. He felt desolate. When he looked up, he found Terry standing there looking down at him.

"How can I leave you all at this stage?"

"It's your Transition that matters, Tony, and that will never leave you now. We expect to return to London eventually and then you can continue on your path with us. I think you have to go with him. It would cause trouble for all of us if you tried to refuse. The Beyond has forewarned us of such a happening. After all, that is how your Transition name arrived. You are truly Nehemiah now, going ahead to rebuild our temple for the homecoming of us all. And Moses has to go with you."

Tony stood up and wandered over for a few words with the group members who were around. He rolled up his little bundle of belongings and came back to The Suit.

"Okay, Tonto. Let's go."

Johnny and a girl who had had enough of mosquito bites and malnutrition came with him and climbed into the back of the steaming hot taxi. Tony looked out of the window with tears in his eyes. He thought about the journey he had been on with The Transition and what his life would be like now, without them. He remembered Terry's words and held on to them. He hoped he was right and The Transition would never leave him. He would never be part of The Beige again. He was outside and beyond all that. He must be, he had to be.

It was a long sweaty miserable journey: taxi, bus and flight out of Honduras but, eventually, they were strapped into seats on a night flight and Mexico City's lights dropped away beneath them. Tony was amused to find they were accompanied by some kind of agent.

"Look," he said to him," you can go to sleep, we're not going to make a run for it at thirty thousand feet."

Chapter Twelve

Unfixable Bethan

The summer term was almost over. Thinking things through on the train, after George had made his decision, I realised that some sort of accommodation had to be made over the summer holiday or I would lose Bethan. Although I was knocked off my feet every time I saw Psyche, I still felt a bit of an imposter in the Floating World. And...she was a lovely, lovely girl, but she wouldn't go all the way with me.

I was trying to exert some control over things that were just too volatile, too unpredictable for me to pin down. Liverpool and Bethan were much clearer to me, or so I thought as we rattled out of Crewe. But I felt, at the same time, that I was probably kidding myself. This was what I later came to call bloke thinking. There is a difficulty, a problem around choice and direction? Okay. Now then: what's the solution? What can I fix?

Well, I sure as hell couldn't fix Bethan. We arranged to meet in a relatively quiet pub. We got so cross with each other that heads turned our way. We left the pub and walked down to the Mersey.

"How many times do I have to tell you? No, I have not been sleeping with her. Yes, I do care about all of them, and yes, George did want to know what I thought he should do."

"So you're telling me that a sophisticated and successful business-man needs to talk to a first year student about how to manage his own son, you're telling me that his beautiful daughter has nothing to do with your jaunts down there?"

"Yes, he did."

"...and...?"

"No, goddammit, she's a good friend of mine, and..."

"Have you had your hands on her?" Bethan's entirely justified jealousy was reaching melting point. I had to answer quickly and dishonestly. Sidetrack.

"Look, Bethan, we are not lovers. And I am not going to be hauled over the coals by you any more. How would you like it if I cross-examined you about...about your close friendship with Jed?"

This was a wild card, and not a good one.

"I'm not up and down to London like a fucking yo-yo in order to see Jed. He's simply one of our crowd and a good pal. You know that perfectly well."

"He took you out when I wasn't here one weekend."

"Well I was fed up and cross with you...and there were four of us."

She did look a little less sure of herself, and I think she did quite fancy Jed.

"And? Did you find him snoggable?"

"He kissed me goodnight, that's all."

Bethan was an openhearted, kindly, honest sort of girl and I was tiring of the grubby game I was playing. She looked disconcerted.

She added fiercely "What do you expect if you leave me for the lights of London, the allure of Kensington?"

She made a fine sneer out of "allure."

At that time, people were not talking about so-called 'open relationships' with more than one partner, as opposed to two-timing. At least, not in Bethan's home environment, nor in mine. I certainly didn't have the strength of character to offer her any such arrangement and anyway, she would probably have told me to stuff it. Besides, I didn't really know where I was headed with Psyche, except that she loved me. And I loved her. And Bethan. But...differently. I looked glumly at the dark water and the lights of Birkenhead. A heavy silence lay between us. Time for some bloke-speak.

"I'm not going to stop seeing George and his family. Tony will be back from Honduras sometime and I want to see him, I'll want to know where his head is at. And actually, it is sort of flattering to have George ask me about Tony and The Transition. And it'll be fascinating watching Psyche's singing career develop. So it'd be great if you could accept that."

"And watch you sail away with Psyche over the summer holidays?"

Aha.

"Au contraire. Why don't you and I sail away? Or hitch off somewhere, at least."

"Are you serious?"

She looked hard at me, trying to work out if this was a bluff to get my own way.

I suddenly realised that, yes, I was serious.

"I've got a few quid stashed away from working in the bar, and if we youth-hostel it, we can get by. Would the Good Doctor and your Mum let me whisk you off for three or four weeks?"

"Come and ask them; I think it'll be ok, but maybe best if you talk about buses and trains and not hitching." She was still watching me, weighing up my offer and her feelings.

Her face cleared. "I'd love that, Gerry, really I would. I've been nowhere except North Wales and Merseyside. Oh, and Lytham Saint bloody Anne's."

"Oh, I've been everywhere, man. Surbiton, Brighton, Portsmouth. All over the Deep South. Hitching, too, so I know what it's like." The confidence of inexperience. I had much still to learn about life On The Road.

"What's it like, then?"

"Pretty horrible sometimes, but when it goes well, it's...exhilarating. And free."

"Iawn. In fact, grêt."

She grabbed me and held me close, kissing me hard and long. As I held her in my arms I knew once again that I didn't want to lose her. And I remembered Psyche's ardent words: "Don't choose. Just go on loving me." I didn't have to choose. Not yet, at any rate.

Bethan's father didn't like the sound of my summer holiday suggestion one little bit. We were over there for Sunday dinner and a stroll, not long before I was due home, so we had to try to settle the idea with him.

"How will you travel?" he asked almost at once. "There seems to be a plague of hitchhiking breaking out."

"We'd rather go by train or bus, really," I said. "Hitching might be necessary if..."

"If?"

"Well, you know, if we missed the last train out of somewhere, or – "

"So you are contemplating hitch-hiking at night with my daughter?"

I just couldn't get my fox-trot right with Doctor Jennings. I sighed. Bethan stepped in.

"I think all Gerry's doing, Dad, is making sure he doesn't promise something he can't deliver. He can't swear we'll never hitch a lift. Sometimes lifts crop up when you're staying in a youth hostel, it's not all standing by the roadside in the rain."

Quite a lot of it is, I thought. I waited for his reply. Answer came there none. I broke the increasingly tense silence.

"But other things being equal..."

"They rarely are, I find. What do you mean?"

I paused. This wasn't the first futile argument I'd had with him and it was embarrassing.

"I mean simply that we would always prefer train or bus."

"Do you have any money?"

Abruptly, Bethan got cross.

"Are you going to means test him? He's offering me a trip abroad. I've never done anything like that."

She left hanging in the air the thought that her parents had never taken her anywhere much. Shrewd, but I was worried it could get nasty. I had to wind this one down quickly.

"As it happens, Doctor Jennings, I've saved up quite a bit from working in the bar."

"What's 'quite a bit?' Enough to take care of yourselves?"

I sighed again. "What can I say? Yes, and if we were to, you know, get in a financial jam...I'd send home, I'm sure my parents would bail us out."

He looked down, and flushed a little.

"And so would we. I'm not trying to insult you, Gerry, but you must expect Bethan's mother and me to be anxious about this idea. If anything happened to her I'd never forgive myself."

I managed to look him right in the eye.

"Do you think I would? She's the world to me."

He looked at me and for the first time I think we actually connected.

"Yes, I can understand that. But you aren't an experienced traveller abroad, are you?"

"I've been to France and Holland, with my family and with a school trip. I've travelled around this country a bit."

It went on like this for another few minutes, until I found myself saying "Your daughter is quite a girl. A strong character. She'll look after me as much as I'll look after her."

That seemed to change our dance a bit.

"Yes. I mustn't underestimate her. I'll talk to my wife and see... see what's to be done."

I was nervous about the fact that we intended to travel across Europe together without being married. But then, of course, he had prescribed the Pill for her. Surely he could hardly have expected her to remain celibate.

He was clearly uncomfortable with the whole idea, and the best thing we could do was to leave him to it for a while. Mrs Jennings' view would probably be crucial. Despite her mild manner, I had come to realise that she often had the final word on how their daughter was raised.

Bethan took me for a stroll on the prom and the beach. She said, a little sharply, "We'll leave him to stew a bit."

"Well, what sort of a dad would he be if he didn't worry?"

"Mum'll sort him out."

And so she did. It was all quite formal.

"Gerry, we're prepared to agree to this adventure for Bethan, but I have some concerns. We both do." Mrs Jennings looked at me and smiled a complicit smile. It was my first insight into how so many men need to maintain a decisive front, behind which their wives actually make things happen. My family had never worked like that.

"We want you to promise a few things."

I risked a jest because I was so pleased they were letting her go.

"So what is your prescription for the holiday, Doctor Jennings?"

He wasn't amused, of course. "It's not a prescription. It's a set of conditions."

I had to promise not to hitch-hike unless there was no safer alternative, to contact them in the event of difficulty or hardship, and so on. All perfectly sensible. Most of them I agreed to in bad faith, knowing we would break our word. "Male chauvinist" was the phrase emerging at the time to describe the way Doctor Jennings made me promise things that applied equally to his daughter. I was the male leader of our holiday, who would handle all the tricky stuff while Bethan applied suncream and looked decorative. Anyway, I was pleased. Much easier for me to break my word than for Bethan.

And that is how we came to spend a night sheltering in some bushes on the outskirts of Calais. Ferry ports were notoriously difficult to hitch out of, with many young people all trying to head inland. The youth hostel was full. Not a glamorous start to our trip, but the next morning we started early. As we climbed into the cab of a truck, the sense of freedom and adventure was exhilarating. "Where you go?" asked the driver. We didn't really know. "Greece," said Bethan, "the islands," and looked at me with a big grin. "Yeah, that's it," I beamed back at her. And that's where, eventually, we landed up.

Bethan was a wonderful travelling companion. She was resilient, eager for new discoveries, good humoured. Naturally we bickered occasionally, but not for long and usually not to any significance. Because I was sometimes anxious about my lack of hitching experience, I would over-extend myself, offering answers I didn't really have. That is, I bullshitted and she was forgiving about it.

"I thought you said it was okay to hitch on the approach to an autobahn."

"Well I'm sorry, Bethan, I was told it was, but look, it wasn't a big fine, was it?"

"Duw, now he's made of money. Perhaps Dad was right," squeezing my hand so I took her only a little seriously. And almost too late, we developed an eye for signs of real danger.

In Serbia, two o'clock in the morning, the truck driver pulled over. It was time to rest up and carry on tomorrow. He indicated that when I had "finished with the girl," I should pass her on to him. He climbed into his neat little bunk behind the front seats.

"Not an appealing prospect," Bethan muttered.

I realised abruptly that I should have suggested she wear a fake wedding ring. In more socially conservative parts of the world, an assumption might be that she was easy, possibly a prostitute. I felt dread rising inside me.

"She won't," I said. I was getting nervous. He was a large man. He stuck his moustachio'd face between the seats.

"Come," he said a little hoarsely to "the girl," ignoring me.

"No," she said quietly, "I don't want to."

A short and intense silence, as he stared at us. I could see rage and disappointment flushing his face.

"Get - YOU - get...OUT. GO!" he roared in our faces.

We did, rapidly.

As we slammed the cab door shut, he got back in the driving seat, started his truck up, swung back on to the road and thundered off.

We laughed, but we were shaken. We looked round. Twilight, a country crossroads, not much traffic.

"Well, it's nice to be wanted, but not my type."

"And if he had been your type?"

Bethan laughed. "Well, you never know."

"Never know? What…?

"Are we living for kicks on this trip? Or are we not?"

"Christ. What sort of kicks would it have been for me, listening to him and you grunting away just behind me?"

She looked up into my face. The laughter had gone from her. She paused, and then:

"You don't own me." Her voice calm and level.

"Well of course I don't, but…"

She flushed up. Her face was tight.

"In the light of…recent conversations and absences, Gerry, you might want to back off just now."

"What the fuck has that got to do with it?"

"EVERYTHING." She shouted in my face. I stepped back from her.

"I'm sorry. But…look …" Her words tumbled out. "You take me for granted, that…I'll be there when you get back from London, you're happy enough then to climb over me and …"

"And WHAT," I yelled.

She stopped, took a breath, and looked at me. Then she giggled.

"And then we go looking for your teeny weeny willy."

"Maybe the lorry driver had a bigger willy, is that it?"

"We'll never know. We could start some comparative measurements, all the way across Europe…" she moved closer. My mouth went dry.

We ended the dispute up against a big pine tree. Long may it flourish. Afterwards, we talked about what the lack of a ring might suggest to an unsophisticated truck driver with limited English.

"That could have ended very badly."

We got a short lift in a local van to the nearest town and caught a train out of Serbia.

A beach life for three weeks was a revelation to both of us. We did some island-hopping, until we settled on Rhodes. We slept on the beach, just a groundsheet and sleeping bags. A fig tree grew at the back of our little cove, under a low cliff, and in the heat of the day we lurked in the shade, and splashed around at the sea's edge to cool down. There were very few people around. A couple of villagers came along, just to see who we were, and they came back with a watermelon. A policeman came by, but really, he was checking that we were safe and not just a couple of naive idiots – which we were.

I read translations of modern Greek poets, Henry Miller's "Colossus of Maroussi," and Lawrence Durrell's books on Cyprus and Rhodes. Bethan read bits of the books to me as I lounged in the shade feeling fortunate, possibly even smug. She was happy reading aloud and didn't want to plough through whole books herself.

The main tourist beach was on the other side of the little town and, as the light faded, we wandered into town to eat at one of the outdoor cafes, ravenous at the smell of lamb and rosemary grilling. The little white houses in the brilliant light helped to smooth out our senses, so we felt unusually at ease with ourselves and each other. The past faded from us in the heat and light. This was life in the present tense.

We had very little money, so I did a few days of washing dishes and Bethan cleared tables. Part of our pay was an evening meal. The owner of the restaurant was quite demanding, insisting we turned up promptly, clearly failing to recognise the true nature of our free-spirited lives. He fancied Bethan so much you could see that it hurt, but by now she had a phony wedding ring on her finger. We had learned our Serbian lesson. Eventually, he introduced us to his family. His wife plainly thought Bethan ought to be wearing more clothes. Their two little boys grinned a lot. The family spoke almost no English. "Deutsch?" they said. Our Greek amounted to no more than "efharisto poli," but that, plus plenty of smiles and gestures, seemed enough.

They offered us a couch to sleep on, but we made them understand we were happy on the beach. At night, we sometimes swam naked, which for northerners like us was an unfamiliar and powerful aphrodisiac. One such night was alive with bioluminescence, when you splashed and swirled in the water. I was out first and I watched Bethan rise out of the shallows with glittering cold sparks running off her body. My feelings were unutterably intense. In such ways, this holiday was more like a honeymoon.

One day as we came into work, the restauranteur looked worried. He pointed at the sky, which was the usual achingly brilliant and empty blue, and made rumblings and zigzag gestures. He pointed into his home and made the universal sleeping gesture, head on one side resting on hands together. We thanked him and I ran back to the cove to collect our things, lugging both rucksacks up the track to the village. We worked our shift, but there was no sign of a change in the weather. Was something a little odd, perhaps scary, developing here? But we did as he suggested and settled down in their living room. The boys emerged and insisted on playing cards with us until their dad came and told them off. "Back to bed," he was obviously saying.

We used their toilet and washbasin and I was walking back to bed when a huge flash lit up the room for a split second, followed by a mighty crash of thunder and a squeak from Bethan, who hated thunder and lightning. I climbed in and held her tight. The storm flashed and crashed for an hour or more and the rain was intense. The wind came in behind the rain, and we didn't sleep a lot.

The next morning it was cooler and the village was sodden and steaming. The sky was a streaky grey and there were real grown-up waves breaking on the beach. It was starting to feel like the end of summer. We chatted over coffee and decided to head for home. The patron and his lady tried to persuade us to stay, and we felt spoiled and fussed over. We wavered, they were such kindly people, and then decided. It was late August, we'd been away a month and it was a long road home.

As it happens (how does it happen?) Tony was also experiencing a rather more boisterous storm that same night in late August.

The train from Thessaloniki to Skopje was heaving. We practically had to fight to get on board. We burst into a compartment to find a young Englishman stretched out across one of the seats. Bethan stared at him. "Weary soldier going home on leave," he said, and smiled graciously, indicating the two remaining places opposite. He got up and slid the compartment door shut. We squeezed in next to an elderly couple, who smiled and nodded. Bethan muttered something to me about chinless ex-public-school twats. He put his nose back in his book and ignored her.

To our delight, the door crashed back, and out of the turmoil in the corridor, a family tumbled into the compartment. A large woman with a toddler on her arm took one look at the weary soldier, reached down and swept his feet off the seat. She sat down and smiled cheerfully at him. He squeezed himself as far from her as he could and became even more fascinated by his book. Her husband came in with another, older kid, and they established themselves with much shuffling of bottoms and rearranging of clothes and parcels. Soon they were passing round snacks and sweets and chatting to anyone who would or could answer. Bethan and I became firm friends with them. Mum pointed at Bethan's ring finger, clapped and laughed, and pointed to her children, with a look that said "and you?" Bethan blushed and shrugged "I don't know." The mum laughed with delight and pointed at me. "No goot?" More loud laughter and she opened a bottle of beer.

In Skopje, the signs of the terrible earthquake of two years earlier were everywhere and the station clock, stuck at the time of the disaster, was eloquent. As we walked away from the station, we saw an old woman shuffling along, bowed under a huge bundle of sticks. She looked as though she had walked out of a different century.

We were lucky with our lifts. A big truck, with a gentle driver, took us through Belgrade in the middle of the night. In the small hours, he pulled into a garage forecourt, indicated we should stay put, climbed over into his little bunk and was soon snoring. We dozed. In the early-morning light, we opened the cab door as quietly as we could and slipped out to pee behind the buildings. When we came back to the truck, "our" driver was standing there looking round anxiously for us. I can still remember his kindly face.

Coffee and a bun, which he bought for us, and then back on the road. There was such tenderness in the way some people decided to help us along, even protect us. We were a young married couple, who clearly were adventurous and either mad or naïve. Why else would we travel like this?

We caught a train in Zagreb and landed up sleeping in the corridor crumpled up against each other, a little too close to the toilets. I woke after being trampled on yet again, and stood to look out of the window. There were my first Alps, shining white against a sky full of stars. It was worth putting up with the stink.

Cars all the way from Munich, once we'd got out of town. More than once, the driver would stop at a petrol station and walk around trying to get us the next lift. One woman, with excellent English, told us her son was off hitching and that was why she had picked us up.

"Where do you live?"

"Dachau," she answered.

I made no comment and a little gap appeared in the conversation. She looked quickly across at me, and smiled warily.

"It is actually a pleasant town...now."

She was perhaps in her mid-forties. So she'd been my age as the war swirled and thundered around her. I realised that she had a head full of stories that I couldn't get at, which was true of so many older people we encountered, at home as well as across Europe.

In Aachen, the old chap in the bar was well into his beers, and insisted on buying us supper. He had been in a Panzer regiment, and was prone to bursts of the "Horst Wessel" song. He would stop himself with "Nein, nein - all friends now, friends," and link arms with us. He'd been robbed of his pension on the way home a month earlier and insisted on walking us in the direction of the youth hostel. "Not safe. Aachen. Many bad people."

"It's late," protested Bethan, "not safe for you too." He reminded us he'd been a Panzer driver, and stuck his chest out. Then he had a fit of the giggles. "All friends now." We reached his block of flats, and he eventually got his key into the lock, hugged us both, and lurched through the door. There was a little balcony to a first-floor window. A light went on, the door crashed open and our friend leaned over the balcony railing, shouting "Friends! Tommy and Jerry, all friends!"

Bethan turned to me with tears in her eyes.

"What he must have seen."

"What he must have done," I countered, then felt bad, so I said, "All friends now, though. Truly." That felt better.

We decided to head straight for Ostend, if we could get a night ride. We wanted to get home now; a return journey picks up a particular momentum and I reckoned the ferry port might only be three or four hours away. We slogged along with our packs. A light rain started, which may have actually helped us get a lift. A middle-aged man in a big shiny car pulled over. "Going where?"

"Ostend for the ferry."

"Please join me. I must drive, not sleep. I want talking to."

Sounded like a deal, though perhaps a slightly dangerous one.

Bethan climbed in the back. I talked to him about...anything. I watched him closely for signs of fatigue, but he seemed to be doing okay. I could hear Bethan snoring quietly in the back. I did the first hour and a half, then I leaned back, prodded her, said "Your turn," and fell instantly asleep.

I woke as we were in the outskirts of Ostend. Bethan and our driver were getting on famously and I felt ludicrously jealous.

He pulled over outside a block of flats.

"Here I stop."

We thanked him profusely, he thanked us profusely, and we wandered off. When we reached the prom, we were a good half-mile away from the port.

"I'm still half asleep," I said. I looked around. There was a half-finished building set back from the road. It was still dark. "Let's shelter. No ferries yet."

The next morning, we walked along the prom in the dawn. A high, bright sky, a fresh breeze off the North Sea. We were half-asleep still, dusty, dirty, and hungry. I don't think I've ever felt so free.

Chapter Thirteen

Homecomings

We arrived at my home during opening hours. The bar was quiet and as I walked in, I felt as though I had been away for years.

My parents were welcoming and inquisitive; they had not met Bethan before. For the next few days we cleaned up and washed clothes. I worked in the bar while Bethan chatted with my father and some of the regulars. She was a bit of a hit.

"You could do a lot worse," said my father one evening as he locked the doors. He was not a man for over-exuberant praise.

After a couple of days and a phone conversation with Mrs Jennings, we headed for North Wales, hitching to Chester and then catching the bus.

"Thank you for the three postcards," said the Doctor pointedly.

"Three? We sent four or five at least."

"Perhaps they'll get here eventually," said Mrs Jennings. "The important thing is that you're back, safe and sound."

"Did you explore ancient Greece? After all, you are studying history."

"Well, I'm more Stalingrad than Salamis, really. Though we had a look at Knossos. Luckily the Minotaur wasn't in. Mostly we studied the beach, the sea..." And each other, I thought, looking across at Bethan, who smiled and looked down. Phosphorescence.

"And did you hitch..."

Mrs Jennings cut in, almost sharply.

"No need to cross-examine him. They are safe home, Gerald managed the travel perfectly well, obviously. It's wonderful to see you both back and looking so well. Did you have a good time?"

"It was...just wonderful, Mum. A big education. So many different sorts of people."

During my couple of days with them, I managed to avoid any more snarky conversations with Doctor Jennings. He worked hard and long, so he was out of the way a lot. I did manage to remember to thank both of them for agreeing to our adventure. Looking back on it years later, I realised how troubling it must have been for them.

I went home and worked in the bar. On my way south, I realised that for weeks I'd hardly thought at all about Psyche, Tony and George. Then I saw the triumphant headlines.

"Cultists repatriated - but who pays?"

"Teenage utopians return to reality."

A scrawny, scruffy Tony scowling at the camera, shoulder-length hair; I would not have recognised him, would have walked straight past him in the street. The press were more interested in the teenage girl.

I sat in the bar listening to the after-closing-time gossip and managed to keep my mouth shut. I knew I had to get up to Kensington and see how they were, before I headed back to Liverpool.

The familiar second-floor door and a tightening in my chest. They had a new-fangled phone doorbell arrangement, which I fumbled. I felt more tense about seeing Tony again than I did about seeing his sister.

George opened the door to me, and smiled his gentle smile.

"How good to see you. Come on in. It's only me I'm afraid, Psyche is auditioning."

"And Tony?"

I followed him over to the table. He poured me a drink, and then himself. He sat down and spread his hands on the table and looked at them for a good few moments, then slowly looked up at me.

"Not going so well, Gerry."

Was he going to cry? I couldn't stand that, so I jumped in.

"Is he okay? How's his health?"

"He looks a lot better than that newspaper photo. He's eating properly."

George ran out of things to say.

"I'm sorry. I mean, my advice..."

"Was eminently sensible. He has been in danger. In fact many of them had a very narrow escape." He told me in brief about the night of the hurricane and Tony's journey home.

"Is he angry with you?"

"It's odd. I thought he'd be furious. You know how he likes his own way. But he wasn't, he's just remote, separate. Polite, and absent."

"Is he living here?"

"No. He is staying, kipping, you might say, at The Transition house. They've taken over more of the building and he has given himself the role of preparing it for the return of the rest of them. He says his Transition name is Nehemiah...no, nor do I, but we can look it up."

We talked and talked, about Tony, the school, The Transition in general and Terry in particular, Psyche's singing, but mostly we talked about Tony. George was still the same soft-spoken, cool presence, but he seemed to have wilted a little. He glided off into the kitchen and knocked up some supper so we didn't get too drunk. Well, George didn't.

"Do stay over, Gerry." Perhaps he had no one else to talk to like this. I felt pleased and flattered to be of use to him.

He answered my unasked question. "I don't think she'll be back tonight; the audition is in Cardiff."

"I told Tony I'd look after her, George, and I haven't been here for either of you."

I think he could see I was on the edge of getting maudlin. I was a sloppy sort of drunk.

"She's fine, she had a nice break in France, she's into her final year and her singing is going very well."

I slept in Tony's room - or what used to be Tony's room.

Late the next morning, after a stroll in the park, I decided to take my hangover up to Liverpool. I asked George to tell Tony and Psyche I'd be down to see them soon, and George held on to my hand when I shook it.

"You are a good friend to us all Gerry, and I hope to see you before too long."

I felt ridiculously proud.

"And I'll see who's on at Ronnie's."

Even better.

Just sometimes, and with no prompts, life unrolls a scene that could have come from an old-fashioned romantic movie. I was walking across the pavement outside Euston when I had to stop, take off my rucksack, put it on the ground and get out my wallet and ticket. When I looked up, Psyche was in front of me. I moved towards her, stumbled over my rucksack and fell into her arms, so she was holding me up. We were both laughing as I untangled my feet. I pushed her gently back so I could look at her.

"You look bloody marvellous," I gushed.

She laughed again. "You're not too bad your suntanned self."

We hugged and kissed with people hurrying all round us. We collected a wolf-whistle or two.

"How come you...?"

"George told me your train time."

Over a coffee we agreed that we'd both had good summer trips. Her Cardiff audition had seemed to go well. She told me a little more about Tony's alienated, strange state of being. She asked about Bethan. I told her about my duels with Dr Jennings. I unkindly played up how square he was, just to make her laugh. I did like watching her laugh, it hadn't happened all that often.

What we didn't talk about was Psyche and Gerry.

"Please come back down and see us again soon. I know Tony will be pleased to see you."

"And you?"

She paused, looked at me, put her hand behind my head and kissed me long and hard. Tongues. A waitress came over and told us to cool down or clear off. We both blushed, and I had to wait a little before standing up.

She walked me to my platform. We stood and looked at each other.

"Remember," in a low voice, "I love you. It's okay about Bethan. Don't choose. Just come and see me. Us. Soon. Please?"

"Oh, gosh, very well, if you insist...look, of course I will. Gotta go."

A peck on my cheek, and she was walking away from me into the crowds.

I sat on the train in turmoil. "Don't choose" simply meant two-timing Bethan.

Tony/Nehemiah did not return home in a happy state. He wrote me a letter:

No point in carrying this rage around inside me. I want to be with the others, I want to follow The Transition way, I want to sit with them and touch the Beyond. My father's lawyers have put a stop to that. He can't help it - that's what Beige people do. They follow the usual constraints of their blindness. Even if they are a dad. Particularly if they are a dad.

I couldn't stay in the flat for long. It was good to see Psyche safe and well, but like Dad, she was the other side of the glass. No sign yet of you. Apparently you took Bethan off to Greece over the holiday. You could've come with me, Transitioned alongside me.

I got the key to Number 30, as instructed by Terry, and the money for the work flows in somehow. The place is getting cleaned up. Coffee bar in the basement still. The builders and fitters are very curious, but I turn their questions aside. It's easy to do so and it makes me feel mysterious and strong.

It's good to feel useful to the Elect, but I hate being out of contact with them. No guidance from Terry on how to interpret events. No sense of one Body, one Thought, one Being.

I am Nehemiah, rebuilding the Temple for the great Return. But I wasn't held in exile in the Persian court, I was with my people in the wilderness, following the Way and the Truth, in touch with the Spirit of Ages, the great Beyond.

Sorry to bang on, Gerry. It helps me to write out my mission like this. I can't talk to anyone else about it.

Back to work. Come and see me soon, you boring little jerk!

Three weeks or so after my little bit of Euston Station passion, or "pash" as people sometimes still said, I saw from the papers that the rest of The Transition group were drifting back to London. The press loved it, of course, and so did some of my friends.

"So you're mates with this bunch of crazies and losers, eh Gerry?"

"One of them is my oldest school friend, he's a really interesting bloke."

"Really? Sounds to me like he's a bit off his head. And who is this Nemmeyer anyway?"

I felt weary, couldn't be bothered to go into it all. Such a different world.

"Don't really know. Isn't it your round?"

There were accusations of abduction and brain-washing from enraged parents, dismissive rebuttals from Transition leaders, and – most interestingly of all – a feature about their refurbished and enlarged HQ, being prepared for their return by "Brother Nehemiah." A furious rabbi objected to "this crew of mind-benders" using the name of a leader of the people of Israel.

Tony responded, in a radio interview, "I hadn't realised the Lord exercised copyright."

I dropped Psyche a postcard that simply said "What a to-do! You and George okay?" She answered, "Yes, but when are you coming down?"

I had moved out of hall and shared a revolting terrace house with three other blokes. At first, our girlfriends tried to organise us on a clean-up rota. Mostly, it didn't work. Bethan said crisply that if we wanted to live like pigs, it was up to us. I didn't really want to live in a student sty, but neither did I want a running battle with the others.

In the process of trying to clean us up, Bethan found Psyche's postcard and blew up. I tried all the obvious points: that they were my friends going through a crisis, that I liked them, they mattered to me, I didn't interfere in her friendships, and no, I hadn't slept with her on the way up here, she was in Cardiff. I think the truth of it was still hidden from both of us.

Post-Euston, I wasn't on the same warm vibe with Bethan as I had been. People give out so many tiny signals all the time and our conscious awareness may not register them. It wasn't so much that I was "going off" Bethan; I was simply confused and she felt it.

"Don't make me choose between friendship and love, Bethan."

"Oh for Chrissakes. It's simple enough. Do you love me?"

"Yes." No hesitation.

"Then stop sniffing round your would-be opera singer and her crazy brother and stay here with me and your friends."

My turn to blow, or at least to simmer a bit.

"She's not a would-be, she's very good. She auditioned for the Welsh National Opera. And I'm afraid Tony may be going crazy. Wouldn't you want to help a friend who was cracking up? I'm not going to stop visiting them. Look, I'm sorry Bethan, but you'll just have to get used to it."

"Fuck off to London then."

In her distress, she was gasping her words out.

"Don't expect to come back to me when you...with your cock sticking out...or should I say hanging out..."

That was an unkind reference to our last lovemaking, which had not been successful on my part. It hurt, but it made me see how upset she was. It really wasn't like her.

Her pretty, round face was pink with outrage.

I suddenly felt tired to my bones.

"Bethan. Did we have a lovely summer?"

"Yes, of course," she muttered, looking at her feet. "Do you want me to keep saying thank you?" Her chin came up.

"Bloody hell, no. I just want to stop rowing with you whenever I go to see my friends in London."

"If I didn't care about you, I wouldn't make a fuss. Love makes people jealous sometimes, you know." Tears were running down her cheeks.

I felt like a complete shit. I went to hug her. She turned round and walked off, shaking her head.

Back in my room, I interrogated my miserable and guilty self. It was unreasonable of Bethan to try to stop me going to London to see the Palmeras. But why was I so caught up with Psyche? Bethan had just showed me how much I meant to her. Was that it? Did I feel suffocated, or trapped? No, because I wasn't. How much did Tony really mean to me? A lot. How much did Psyche really mean to me? Unanswerable. Round and round it all went. Abruptly, a quote popped up: "O, reason not the need." I couldn't think rationally through my desires and hopes. Perhaps reason, fairness and morality weren't up to the forces buffeting me. Or was that simply a cop-out? Perhaps I should just make up my mind and choose. Can I choose? No.

So I did what blokes often seem to do. I went out on the town with "the lads" and got very drunk. I shouted and sang very loudly and collected a very firm telling-off from a policeman. I rounded the evening off by throwing up by the pier-head and going to sleep for an hour on a bench, till a mate woke me up. He was shaking my shoulder and telling me it was risky. He led me home and I woke up ten hours later.

A night on the town had generated no fresh insights, it merely left me feeling ill. Why did it take me so long to understand that this recurrent pattern of behaviour was futile? Whatever the intrinsic delights of a good booze-up, they didn't yield any fresh insights into my own situation. It took me years to take this realisation on board.

It being 1965 moving towards 66, it was only a matter of time before other drugs suggested different routes through to different states of being. At least they didn't make me throw up.

Chapter Fourteen

Tony Under the Stars

B ethan wasn't very interested in seeing me after our row. I had a heart-to-heart with one of her closest friends over a pint and she told me that Bethan didn't want to lose me but felt I needed to make a choice.

"It's not that simple..."

"Never seems that simple for blokes, somehow, does it?"

"Look, the two choices aren't in any way equal, it's really not that simple. I'm close to the whole family in London."

"Yeah, right..."

"Look. For the twentieth time, Psyche and I aren't lovers."

Yet, I might have added in hope. And anyway we were, all but.

"Psyche? Is that really her name?" The friend started sniggering.

"And your name is...Eglantine?"

She stopped sniggering. "Okay. Quits."

I came to a small decision, at least. I would not go down to London for a month or two and see how Bethan felt.

Three weeks later, I saw her drunk on the street outside The Crack. She didn't see me. She was with friends and she was crying. I wanted to go to her, I moved to cross the road, but Eglantine was there, saw me, and waved me off. Then I heard she'd been seen around with Jed. Eglantine sent me a note.

"It doesn't mean much. She just wants to see how it feels, to be taken out by someone else. She's testing herself to see how much she still cares about you. You twat."

Fair enough. But I felt jealous and moped around not studying properly, missing indoor cricket training sessions, generally being morose. That's a good way to lose friends as well as a lover, so why was I surprised to find that I felt lonely?

I phoned the flat. George answered. He told me Psyche was doing very well in her final year at music conservatoire and no, he didn't see much of Tony.

"Come on down," he offered. "It'd be good to see you. You can go and talk to Tony. And Roland Kirk is at Ronnie's."

After stopping by at the flat to say hello to George and drop my bag off, I went over to The Transition house in Fitzrovia. Psyche was at the Guildhall working late on some recital songs but I might see her later, George had said.

The Transition house was bigger and more imposing than I'd expected. The front door was open, with workmen carrying in equipment and materials. I called up the stairs and Tony came hurrying down. He took both my hands, then gave me the briefest of hugs. That was a first in my life from a man. It gave me a rush of affection for him and I treasure that memory still.

We found a quiet room free of refurbishing work and he told me, slowly and carefully, what had happened in Honduras. It was so extraordinary that I wrote some of it down, which he didn't seem to mind.

When he moved into Transitionese, I tried to steer him back towards events and feelings, facts and responses. He did his best, I think out of kindness to me, but events, his feelings about them and The Transition were inseparable now. He reminded me of a couple of Marxists I knew in Liverpool: the answers to my questions were clear, why couldn't I see that? Comforting, to be inside an absolute value system. Yet Tony didn't seem comforted; he looked strained, seemed older.

"Let me show you how my range of awareness has extended. You remember my interest in astrology? Come back tomorrow and I'll cast your horoscope, maybe bring the Tarot into it too."

"Great, I'll be round late morning."

"Fine. So don't get too pissed with Dad tonight."

"Come and join us."

He hesitated. "That would be good in some ways, but...not best for all of us at the moment."

I think he meant for himself.

"Okay. See you tomorrow."

After I left, I think he must have spent some hours poring over charts and his own notes. He was certainly ready for me the next day. I pictured him up there in an attic, bent over a table with his charts and star maps, as an astrologer might have done four hundred years previously. A John Dee of our times.

I found this stuff much more interesting than The Transition. That may have just been an aesthetic judgement, or perhaps the fact that the roots of it were ancient and tangled in with the birth of modern science. And it wasn't a closed system with absolute rules, it was an individual search. I walked back to George's flat, looking forward to the next morning. Tony worked on into the night, checking his star maps and charts, laying out Tarot cards several times, scribbling down thoughts and observations. I found some later. They looked like gobbledygook, but they were the basis for what he told me the next morning and that wasn't nonsensical.

Tony told me later he wondered if I would turn up for my horoscope. "You are so obliging, it's hard to tell, but I know you don't usually let people down over an appointment."

"What's it like, doing all this - stuff?"

"Gerry, listen patiently like a good boy and I'll try to tell you."

He paused. "I think you'll probably say I'm off my head...but insights often take people out of their daily selves. I don't think you've ever really accepted that, and..."

"Okay, Magus, get on with it, I'm all ears."

He sat pondering a little, looking down.

"When I sit in stillness and calm, in touch with The Beyond, I can hear the stars whisper and sing as they move, as they sweep in slow majesty across the sky."

He looked up to see if I was listening.

"Go on."

"Well, as they move, infinite numbers of influences, of changes, shift under them. In my mind, I get a growing sense of rightness, of it all fitting together. Then I know I am ready to begin letting The Beyond speak through me, through the stars, through the cards. Then I know how to tell people what they need to know – and I know what they mustn't."

"So, excuse my levity Tony, but it's not just... guesswork? Maybe it's untethered intuition?"

"Intuition is important. That's not the same as guesswork. I can't afford to guess. It has to be in alignment, all of it. Then I, Tony, am not here. Then the star charts, the table, the cards, the elements, the humours, are not really there. And it happens silently."

I was fascinated. The building was quiet, the workmen had gone. There was just a little remote traffic noise and Tony's voice.

"Gerry, you won't hear or see anything out of the ordinary. I shall speak to you in my usual voice. Yet inside me is a sacrament unfolding. True guidance. Into a fuller understanding of who you are, where you stand. And from that understanding, you will know your path."

I wasn't sure about a sacrament, but I kept quiet. His voice grew fainter and less confident.

"I don't really know why I do this. Afterwards, I feel drained, poured away. I don't ask for any money. Actually, I need to think about this. Word will spread. I could quickly be overwhelmed by people who think I'm fortune telling. But I want to do this for you."

At the time I am writing this, we are often described as living through troubled times, with a dangerously uncertain future. That feeling is not limited to this century. When I was at school, the Cold War was a frightening reality and the Cuban missile crisis was an intense tightening of that screw. Through all these threats, young people could still be carefree, the future could seem full of hope. We thought "it" couldn't happen. Yet history shows us it very nearly did, two or three times. Who knows what history will show people in future about the first half of this twenty-first century?

As I wandered through London that evening, I felt the sort of contentment and freedom that I hope young people can still feel sometimes, despite the all too well-evidenced threats to their future. I met up with a couple of ex-Dallinghoo friends. We wandered down to the Earl's Court Road ("Kangaroo Alley") and tried to gate-crash parties full of Australian students and young travellers. Eventually we gave up. I had a couple of pints and went back to the flat comparatively early.

And there she was, lying on the sofa with headphones on and her eyes shut. She was concentrating on the music, frowning.

I came and sat opposite her until she opened her eyes wide, perhaps a little scared for a moment. She sat up and took off her headphones.

"How long have you been sitting there watching me?" She sounded edgy, uncertain.

I smiled at her; I felt wide open to her. "Not long enough."

Her face cleared and she came and sat beside me, holding my hand. "Peeping Tom," she said.

"And some," I answered, and kissed her.

"I was listening to – no, I was learning – the roles of Dorabella and Fiordiligi. I've had a recall for the Welsh National Opera. It's only the chorus, before you get too enthusiastic, but it is for "Così," so I want to really get inside the whole thing. I can't reach Fiordiligi with any comfort."

"But you aced Dorabella at college, didn't you?"

She looked pleased and embarrassed. I loved the way her customary cool broke down at such a moment. I kissed her again, with a little more urgency. She broke off.

"Where's George?" I asked, thinking his presence might be inhibiting her.

"Oh, he's out. Look, I'm sorry, Gerry, but I really do need to carry on studying the opera, and I've got another three to… inhabit before next Thursday."

I probably looked sulky.

She watched me a moment. She smiled and said, "Anyway, you smell of beer and cigarettes." I pushed her over, she laughed and swung a kick at me and I wandered off into Tony's old room. I had laughed too, but I felt she was making a point. I couldn't just roll up and expect her to stop everything for me. I was not to take her for granted, but I wasn't sure I ever had. How could I? I wasn't even sure who she was, or how she would behave towards me next time I saw her.

Which was the next morning. I woke with a start to find her slipping naked into the bed, her eyes full of tears. I lay looking at her in astonishment and then delighted anticipation.

"Just hold me, please."

"Why are you crying?"

"I don't know what to do with you."

I propped myself up on one elbow, and rolled the sheet down off us.

"I can tell you exactly what to do with me," I said, and pointed to my erection.

Such a mistake. She gasped, looked away and almost wailed. "It can't all happen, I'm sorry, it can't...I..."

I did as she'd asked and just held her as she sobbed.

"Are you a virgin? Is that it?"

Her head was on my chest. I felt rather than saw her shake it.

She took my hand and put it where it had been once before. By the time she had climaxed, I'd exploded all over the place.

"Yuk," she said, and slid off to the bathroom.

She came back and lay against me. I felt relaxed, happy, but puzzled.

We shared the cup of tea she'd put by the bed and then I put down the cup. We were sitting up side by side, and I gently turned her face towards me.

"I have to know how it is with you. Look...excuse me being crude, but...is it my cock? Cocks in general?"

Her face was full of pain.

"Yes, I think that's it."

I could hardly hear her.

"I mean, in general..."

A little more loudly: "I'll try being crude and direct too. I think it's cocks in general. It's not just your cock. That's part of you. And I love you. So much. So very much. I just wish... I do love you, Gerry, from top to toe except that bit, that great bobbing, bouncing thing, wobbling away."

This was hard to take. I must have looked crestfallen.

"You being on the planet makes life bearable. I mustn't cling. But I do feel very lonely when you're gone. Back to Liverpool and Her...the mythical, legendary, sensible Bethan..."

She started weeping again. I lay her back down with me and held her tight.

"Look. It's ok. We can just do what we just did. I'm not going to chuck you because you don't want the whole thing. It'll be all right. We'll just be an odd sort of couple that doesn't actually... screw."

I think I meant it, at the time.

As I walked round to The Transition house, a simple fact was gnawing at me. She didn't want me inside her, yet she wasn't a virgin. I worked my way past builders and decorators and found Tony at the top of the house, frowning over his charts. He looked up briefly.

"There you are. You're late."

"I didn't know there was a specific – "

"It's not about your punctuality, you twat. Some times of day are better than others for what we're going to do."

"Right. I'm all ears."

We started with Tony checking my birth-date and time. This he then took to a large map of the zodiac, spread open on the floor, with a few sheets of notes next to it. Then, after a few minutes, he sat down at his table opposite me and just looked at me. I began to feel uncomfortable.

"Do you think I'm going to predict your future?" he asked abruptly. "Because I'm not."

"OK, so what are you going to do?"

"It's what we - both of us - are going to do. We'll discuss possible future events, given all I know of you. Our friendship is a unique opportunity for us to work up something useful to you. Perhaps to me also."

"Well you could do that in the pub, with no charts or anything."

"Your horoscope is a great help. And we'll also consult the Tarot. Maybe, when my studies are further ahead, the I Ching."

"If not about my future, then..."

"I'm going to explore the influences of the heavenly bodies on you at the moment of your birth. That may confirm some of the things you think you know about yourself and contradict others. The history of our friendship will help, so will my understanding of you. We can then interrogate the star chart in the light of a question or two you may have in mind, at that specific moment. It's at this point we move to the Tarot. So we're exploring probability and potential, not defining your future."

I was fairly sure I didn't think the stars and planets had any specific influence me. My scepticism must have showed in my face.

"Just try to suspend your disbelief whilst we do this, Gerry. Like you would in the theatre. You know they're only actors, but they sweep you up in their pretence, until you laugh or cry or whatever, right? Well, if you allow yourself to be swept up, you'll get much more out of this. Let me give you one crossover fact between this belief system and the scientific one from our education. I've read that you can measure the tide, that is, the pull of the moon, in a glass of tap water. And as you know, each us is very largely water. So don't tell me the moon has no influence on our well-being or our feelings."

"I wouldn't dream of it, Tony. Please carry on."

He smiled briefly, but he looked as strained as he had done the previous day.

I could barely follow, and can't now clearly recollect, all the talk he gave me as he sought to relate aspects of my personality to my horoscope. Star signs, the phase of the moon, the sun's movements, planets in trine, planets in opposition, I let it flow around me. There was something hypnotic about it and I fell into a state like the one I still get when I'm in the barber's chair and he's using the comb and scissors. Because Tony knew me so well, there were only one or two aspects where I disagreed with the planets.

"I don't think I'm particularly brave...moral or physical courage...that's maybe why I'm so perplexed in my love life. I'm caught between your sister and Bethan. I'm scared of losing both of them."

"You don't know how brave you are until you are truly tested. Look." More zodiacal jargon, something in opposition to something else in a different house..."This shows us you are powerful with potential courage."

"We'll see."

On we went.

Having more or less agreed that I was the sort of person we both thought I was anyway, and considered my potential for various kinds of action, Tony said we should move across to the Tarot.

I thought then, as I do now, that there's a bit more to the Tarot than to astrology. The Tarot symbols deal with archetypal characters that have rattled around in stories, legends and myths for thousands of years. Who knows how much of it each of us has absorbed and carries forwards? The Fool on the Hill, Dostoevsky's Idiot, The Lovers, the Moon. So as I laid down the cards, trying to allow my mind to be unfocussed, I had some faith that a useful reading might happen.

"It's more a question of what would be the consequences if you did something, rather than what's going to happen to you. That brings your self-knowledge, such as it is, you grinning idiot, it brings your understanding of your own workings at a deep level. It brings it all to bear on the ancient resonances of the Tarot."

I was grinning because our views of The Occult coincided for once, though I didn't and don't think there's anything particularly occult about using the Tarot (or even the I Ching) to explore potential situations and consequences. It doesn't hand everything over to the alignment of stars thousands of light years away.

"Lead on, O Magus."

"And don't take the piss, or I'll have you thrown out."

Vintage Tony; this was going well.

Several times he asked me to lay out the cards in different ways. It was complex, because Tony used the four suits, the Minor Arcana (four of cups, queen of swords) as well as the better-known Major Arcana (The Empress, The Hanged Man.) Each time, I tried to let my mind remain in neutral. Any mindfulness meditator nowadays would find that easier to do than I did back then. They would know not to try hard to think of nothing, and they would know you cannot "empty your mind." Nevertheless, after my astrology head massage, I felt fairly relaxed and neutral.

It took a long time. Tony would pause and look at me thoughtfully for a few moments. Eventually: "Okay. I'm picking up the general picture. I'm going to meditate, see if anything comes through." He meant from The Beyond, I realised.

"I want you to do one final deployment of the cards, thinking calmly and gently about the biggest tangle in your life at the moment and what might happen if you were to resolve it in different ways. Lay seven cards out in a simple horseshoe shape. Do it slowly. I'll be back in ten minutes. It's important you don't turn them over before I return to you."

I can be as sceptical and rational as I like, now. Back then, because of the power of Tony's personality, his knowledge of me, our shared stories, my affection for him and the passion of my start to the day: given all this, I felt removed, remote. A gentle grey light fell on me and on the table, through the grubby window in the roof. I did as he'd asked, and sat back, feeling...I don't know how to describe it. Spaced out, lightly stoned, but these clichés don't describe the sort of calm that had descended. It tickles the back of my neck to think about it, even now. I felt beyond my usual identity. You could say my ego was calmed.

"How you doing?" he asked, quietly.

"Slightly stoned."

"Just right. Turn them over, one by one please, pausing after each."

I'm not going to identify the cards, because I can't remember them all and anyway it was my reading, not yours. But I can't forget The Tower, The Hermit and The Fool. We talked about each card. The Tower was scary, but Tony said that it simply showed what could happen and anyway, it was not just a picture of destruction. It suggested that I could receive a bolt of lighting, a forceful understanding of new realities, different ways of thinking and feeling.

"Remember, Gerry. This isn't fortune-telling. Your actions are yours, generated by you. And what happens as a result, that's simply your karma. Your cards tell us only about potentials and consequences. They answer questions like what if I do this or that."

Then he asked me what tangles were in my mind. I told him, obviously enough, that the difficulties over resolving the pull of Psyche and Bethan were central and that a second knot had crept in unannounced.

He lit up at that. "Shows how well we've been working." The second knot in my soul was about my future employment, my career path.

We talked about each card for a while longer. Eventually he said, "Read your cards to me, in the context of your love-life and your career choices. They are your cards, not mine."

I realised abruptly just how much power he had over me at that moment. He must have felt it.

"Oh, relax. If we can't be straight with each other, this won't work. And what could I do that would harm you, with all this that we're working up here?"

"Well...you could...well, maybe you could tell Psyche, or Bethan, things that..."

He looked cross.

"Who are you?"

I was taken aback. "Gerry, I'm Gerry."

"And I'm Tony, so don't start talking bollocks now, please. This is the difficult stuff. This is the fruit of our labours. Come ON!"

I paused, trying to relax, to get back into that lightly-stoned feeling.

"I think the reading suggests that I have been looking for one resolution, one choice, between these two women" (keep it objective, I told myself, it's his sister) "and there may not be one choice. Perhaps the Hermit is telling me that's how I will end up if I force it, and – "

"Hate to interrupt, but remember, the Hermit also means you have to find your own way, and you can. On your own. Such a search can result in a greater understanding. Doesn't imply you'll land up living in a cave on your own."

"Ah. Okay. That's encouraging. So does that relate to the new ways of understanding that may come to me in a flash? Lightning hitting the tower of my conventional patterns of thought?"

"He's got it. I do believe he's got it."

"Swords?"

"Obvious, isn't it? There may be conflict. If so, it probably won't always be pleasant but it'll be necessary to keep moving. You could easily give up. And remember, you also had in mind your future ways of earning a living."

He looked hard at me. It was almost The Transition stare.

"Have a think, keep looking and feeling. When you're ready, tell me more. But don't try to think hard about stuff - just watch the cards and let them speak to you."

It was as if I could hear things sliding into place, creating patterns.

Eventually, I said, "I think I have to take risks. The Fool is close to the precipice, but I need his innocent, open outlook on the world, that is, his view of my behaviour and that of others. I'll need to fight my way ahead sometimes, and if I go back to beating myself up about choosing between Bethan and Psyche...I will fail. I'll be the two figures falling off the Tower. So...so I should stop worrying about choosing a path. Refusal to choose should be my path. It's like a non-path. No path of my making, at least. The universe will do what it does and I should just dance through it. The consequences of forcing myself, and the girls, into a choice...just won't work."

"Why? That's what the world would generally say. Two-timing is unpopular."

Long pause. Then I found an answer. "As long as both women know what is happening, it isn't two-timing. The consequences of trying to choose are probably destructive. For all three of us. Anyway, the answer may lie entirely in their hands. Why must it be me who tries to control the situation?"

"And your future so-called career?"

"It will just happen to me. Or am I being lazy and just avoiding decisions?"

"Only you can answer that question."

"You look tired, Tony."

"You look washed-out, too. Self-exploration is so demanding, when it's honest."

We arranged to meet for a meal later. As I walked back to the flat, several thoughts came crowding in. The choiceless path with Psyche and Bethan was what Psyche wanted, not Bethan. So be it. Trouble ahead.

Tony hadn't mentioned or suggested I join The Transition, and the cards hadn't spoken of it. That was a relief.

And I wanted some sort of career path to open up for me. I needed to find my own way. The Hermit had to embark on a lonely quest to find his own wisdom.

I stopped walking for a moment. I realised that meant turning down my father's offer to take over the pub. It was an offer I had considered quite seriously. I loved the world of the pub, the easy, boozy sociability, the actual trade and all its "gear, trim and tackle." I'd grown up with beer pumps, shiny clean glasses, casks, bottles, optics, the ring of the till.

"A history honours graduate, running a London boozer?" my mother had once said, which I saw at once rather hurt the old man's feelings.

"Why shouldn't a graduate run a pub? Think of the sparkling conversation from behind the bar," I said, trying to lighten it up. He laughed. "They want to relax and gossip. They want to get pissed in good company. They don't want to know about Bismarck."

Well, now I knew myself better, in this area at least. I wasn't one of the world's natural licensees and I'd have to tell him so. Nothing to do with class or education, it just wasn't me. I realised that I'd be useless at it.

At the flat, there was no sign of anyone, just a note on the table, from her, sealed in an envelope.

Hello, Hand of God. I'm staying late in college and having a drink with some of the other singers on the way home. George is away (again). See you later (perhaps) or tomorrow. Which prospect makes me wet.

A revelation. Direct words about her sexual arousal from a girl. I'd never had anything like that written to me before. Or spoken to me. Bethan might have said, "Good screw last night, you been taking pills, cariad?" But she'd never referred to her own desires in such a specific way.

Tony and I had a subdued meal. The day's energy transfer left us both in a peaceful, flat, strangely satisfied state. He told me a bit more about Honduras, I told him a bit more about life in Liverpool. He didn't tell me to leave university, I didn't tell him to leave The Transition. He did tell me the top hierarchy of The Transition would be focussing on the USA from next year sometime, and that Terry and the Elect were unlikely to stay in London for long even if they did return. The others would filter back in and get the UK effort going again.

Back at the flat, no sign of Psyche. Still out? Asleep? I felt like an intruder and crept quietly off to bed.

Chapter Fifteen

Into The Dark

I stayed down an extra night, and we did go to Scott's. Psyche worked on her opera stuff in the afternoon and I heard her sing a little, which was a delight. Tony stayed away. George came home and ate with us. He seemed diminished, even quieter than he used to be. I watched him a little, surreptitiously, as I thought. Eventually he said, with a sad little smile, "You can stop eyeing me up, Gerry. I'm not ill, I'm concerned about Tony, but I still think I did the right thing."

"You had no choice," was all Psyche said.

"How was he, Gerry, when you saw him?"

"Well, you know I spent much of yesterday with him, and he was in good form. We had a big astrology and Tarot session and all is now clear before me."

Why did I try, at moments of possible tension, to make light of things? Psyche flushed up, and her eyes went wide. I had to say more or she'd be expecting a big announcement, perhaps a final decision.

George and his daughter, in different ways, asked if I actually believed in "all that stuff." My answers were varieties of "I do and I don't." I tried to explain the cultural roots of the Tarot, the state of mind you needed to be in as you lay out the cards, and the way the close relationship I had with Tony gave our findings extra resonance.

It was an interesting discussion, open-minded, civilized and thought-provoking. I did not go into the question of the choiceless choice I'd made between Bethan and Psyche. Instead I used my own employment prospects as the area for not choosing.

Roland Kirk, soon to be Rahsaan Roland Kirk, was at Scott's. It was a sensational, noisy, joyful event. His assorted pipe-and-valve contraptions hung about him. At one point, a man in the audience, exhilarated and probably drunk, high, or both, started interspersing his "Yeah! Yeah!" cries with a range of rich obscenities. Kirk beckoned him down to the stage, urged him to come forward. Eventually, he did, amidst mutters and grumbles from the audience. Kirk felt for the man's hand, held his arm and calmed him right down, telling him it was "all fine, all cool here, we don't need none o'that stuff, just relax and dig it, just dig, you hear me, man? Let's be cool and enjoy ourselves, yeah? Yeah?" Kirk had such a huge warm presence. The man tottered back to his seat calmed and steady.

"You could say that cat's just been Kirked," said Psyche in my ear. Her eyes were shining. "By a magician."

Kirk flipped a flute out of the bell of his tenor, buzzing, singing and roaring through it as he played. We'd heard cool flute often enough. Here was blistering hot, funky flute.

Then back went the flute, up came three horns at once and the one-man horn section took off. Down went two of the horns, out came a fierce tenor solo, back went the rest of the hardware. We loved it, loved him.

A great night. We walked slowly away from the chattering, delighted audience spilling out onto the street. Psyche held my hand tightly. She looked flushed, elated but also perhaps a little taut.

George was out, as he'd said he would be.

"Are you very tired?" I asked.

"Yes...but also, no, not at all."

We went to bed. She said she wanted to try "the whole routine. You've been so patient."

It was a disaster.

She was aroused, and seemed ready, but when push came to shove, I couldn't, because she wouldn't let me. She wailed in desperation.

I felt frustrated and cross, but that faded quickly away, along with my ardour. I lay back and pulled her over on to my chest. She wept on me as I lay thinking through our encounters and what she'd said. It was no use any more saying that it didn't matter because we loved each other. It mattered just because we did love each other.

A terrible, leaden certainty settled over me. I gently sat her up. She knelt among the rumpled sheets and watched me. Her sobs had subsided. Her skin gleamed in the faint light from the windows. This was an image that I knew would never leave me, a moment that would never return. I took a deep breath, and breathed out slowly. I didn't want her to catch my tension.

"Psyche, what happened to you? What has done this to you?"

"I can't..."

"You must. Please. This isn't a free choice you're making, is it? It's something deep. From...when? What is it? ?"

Abruptly, she turned her back.

"Hold me."

George's business associates used to come round to the flat sometimes. They made a big fuss of her and one of them in particular, "Uncle" Billy, offered to take her to concerts, shops, exhibitions. It was exhilarating and flattering.

"How old were you?"

By now her voice was dull and quiet.

"Fourteen. Fifteen."

I could feel the dread rising up around both of us; cold, dark water, pulling her down, trying to silence her. We both knew what was coming.

Her courage was heartbreaking.

Billy was a smooth operator. He moved slowly and gently at first. A little kiss on the cheek. Holding on to her hand a little longer than was necessary. And Psyche was learning how to flirt a little, taking it all lightly, at face value.

"What about your mother?"

"Dead, two years earlier."

"George?"

"Blind. Or turned a blind eye. Uncle Billy was a powerful, wealthy man."

Billy got her used to a little champagne. Got her used to his arm round her waist, showing off to his friends, "Hey, come and say hello to Georgie Palmera's little girl." Got her used to a little dance with him at a club he took her to, "just a gentle waltz"."

One evening he took her back to his place. He'd said, "Just until your Dad gets home."

A little champagne to toast another happy day. A little waltz. Very close-up. She felt his erection and stepped back. He held on to her, with increasing force, and pushed her over.

"Then he raped me. It hurt. He told me I'd led him on. It was my fault. I was a little tart. Lucky to have a man like him. And I was never to tell anyone, or George would suffer and so would I."

She told George. He was horrified, said he'd no idea this could happen. No, she shouldn't go to the police, they'd tell her it was her fault and do nothing. It wasn't her fault, it really wasn't, he said. Such words sat uselessly on the surface.

"Probably best for everyone if you don't tell anyone else."

She never saw "Uncle" Billy again, and the flat was never again filled with George's business accomplices.

From that day, George could hardly look her in the eye.

"So I'm sorry, horribly sorry, my darling Gerry. That is why I don't like cocks."

I was crying and raging. I wanted to kill Billy.

"Now I'm going to my bed. Tomorrow, you must go back to university."

Still a flat, dull voice, a tone I'd never heard from her before and never wanted to hear again.

"And you…I think you will always be the love of my life. But. You must leave here in the morning and never look back."

She was walking towards the door.

"I'm bad for you, Gerry."

The door closed quietly on my tearful protestations of love and devotion, but they sounded hollow to me. At that moment, I knew I couldn't build a life with someone I loved but couldn't make love to. Young people want it all, and all at once, don't they?

The morning after the night before, she didn't wake me in the dawn light with gentle kisses. There was just a note on the table. All it said was "Sorry." She was gone. I was alone in the Floating World of George's flat, scene of adventures and delights, and now of a grey hopelessness. I knew I wouldn't be back for a while, if ever.

I slipped out and bought her some flowers, a little bunch of freesias. I thought of leaving a note. "I'll always love you. Let's stay friends." Then I thought of what it would be like, trying to be just friends with those dark eyes watching me, and I knew such words were phony, except the "always love you," which would probably just hurt her more. She was being unselfish, turning away from someone she loved because she thought she was bad for him. My eyes filled again.

I lay the freesias on her pillow and walked through insubstantial streets to Euston, thinking of her hair on the pillow next to the flowers, thinking...

"Oi! Watch out! Love's young dream," called out the man I'd walked into.

I mumbled my apology and wandered on to the train, feeling tragic, desolate. I was dismayed to find myself thinking that at least this might clear the way back into Bethan's bed. The Tarot and the stars had helped me leave it to fate, and Fate had spoken. Then I realised with sudden shame that there was no equivalent journey for Psyche, no other bed to welcome her.

I did what I've often done when things get too tight across my chest, too heavy on my forehead, when I feel hollowed-out. I went to sleep. I woke up as the train pulled into Lime Street.

I still felt like shit.

Psyche wasn't bad for me, of course. It was herself she was bad for. I guess, nowadays, we could have gone to a sex therapist, or broken the curse of George's secrecy injunction and got her some analysis, or traumatic stress counselling. But most of the time, she didn't behave like someone under great stress. Her deep sadness was what troubled me, and her loneliness, her apartness.

I had little enough insight into my own well-being back then. I should have known that my need for Psyche was more powerful than my desire for penetrative sex with her (to use a contemporary and rather harsh idiom). Other arrangements could have been made and, had it been a few years later, when "open relationships" were common currency, they might have been made. But I took Psyche at her word and stayed away.

From Psyche's revelation until almost the end of my second year at university, I was an embarrassment. For weeks I moped around the city like a cross between Hamlet early in the play and Jacques in "As You Like It." Sometimes I rather enjoyed my melancholy. Without fully understanding why, I felt I needed to have a role, since I was so disenchanted with myself. I read that cynical pessimists don't cheer up and get a grip, because they like things just as they are. But sometimes it was the real thing, a low-key background depression.

After a chance find in a second-hand clothing shop, I took to wearing a wide-brimmed black hat, and someone was silly enough to tell me it suited me. Liverpool can be a windy city, and sometimes I had to scamper down the road after it, which rather spoiled the image. My friends got fed up with my gloomy presence and my too-frequent bouts of maudlin drunkenness. At least I never told them about Psyche and the depth of her pain. They thought for a while it was Bethan I was sad about, and that was true too.

I wasn't sad all the time, of course. Bethan was one of those who told me the hat suited me and that cheered me up. She revolved around the edge of my group of friends. She seemed as resilient, practical and cheerful as she'd been in Greece. I tried telling one friend that I was still getting over the fact that I'd been dumped twice and that I loved both women. He told me to stop being a clown, I'd infuriated Bethan with my London nonsense, and I only had myself to blame.

"Will she come back to me, do you think?"

"You won't know till you try, will you? Might help if you stopped walking around the city like a streak of piss in a black hat."

I bought a long navy-blue wool coat from someone who had gambled too much of his grant away. It was very cheap. The next time I bumped into Bethan, she said, "I've seen you wandering around looking like an anachronism; here's something to complete the illusion." She gave me a big red woollen scarf, and arranged it round my neck and over my back. She stepped back to admire the effect.

"There. Bonsoir, M'sieu Bruant."

"Eh?"

"Look him up. Toulouse-Lautrec. Aristide Bruant."

She gave me a kiss. It was a little more than a peck, a lot less than it would have been months before. Then she stood back and looked at me with her head to one side, smiled at me, and wandered off. I watched her neat little self go down the street, and wondered if I should have told her about her mother's letter, which had arrived a couple of days earlier.

Dear Gerald,

I hope you don't mind me writing to you out of the blue.

I was sorry to hear from Bethan that you two had gone your separate ways. I hope you know that you were and always will be welcome here.

I'm worried about Bethan. One of her cousins is a student at Liverpool, in her third year. She tells me she thinks Bethan is drinking too much, not studying enough and seeing a lot of boys.

I'm not asking you to spy on her, Gerald, and I'm not wanting to be critical about our daughter. Our generation did things differently, but then we were a wartime generation. If you could manage still to be a good friend to her, it would reassure me. It might be best if you didn't tell her I've written to you, and her father doesn't know either. A bit of a secret between you and me, if you don't mind. And no need to write back, it just helps me to know that you've read this. You are a kind and sensible boy.

With kind regards,

Daphne Jennings

I felt a guilty pleasure in holding this secret with Mrs Jennings, or 'Daphne' as now she was to me, and the praises at the end of her letter went straight to my head. Was I kind and sensible? "Well, Daphne," I said quietly into my pint glass that evening, "I will try to be."

"You what?" from the next table.

"Nothing, just - mumbling."

"Well shut up, you gloomy cunt."

Such gross company, I decided, would not suit M'sieu Bruant. I threw my red scarf back over my shoulder, and swept out of the pub. It seems I was the kind of boy a worried mother would share secrets with. Actually, a rather pretty mother, I remembered. The sort of boy who was entrusted with her daughter's well-being. That kind of boy, was I? I felt more confident than I'd done for weeks.

It was agreed amongst a few of my cricketing friends that Bethan had indeed been "seeing" rather a lot of boys. They couldn't make this comment without a certain calculating prurience. I could see some of them were fancying their chances. I poured as much cold water on them as I could.

"Forget it, Euan. She's got good taste. After all, she chose me," splutters of jeering laughter, "and she doesn't like the hairy hulk sort of bloke."

"Well, you'd know about hairlessness, wouldn't you Gerry?"

All good-natured enough, with only a little edge.

Then one evening in the student union bar, as Bethan wandered through en route to the ladies, someone started whistling a few bars from the theme tune of the "Horse of the Year" TV programme. There were a couple of silly grins from some of the blokes. Bethan blushed and tried to ignore them. When she emerged from the ladies, she turned away and left the bar by a side entrance. I was puzzled and troubled. The moment passed, and we drank on, getting loud and silly, as young men do. Then not long before closing time, when some of us were fairly well pissed, one of them whistled the phrase again. I looked at him.

"What's going on?" I asked him.

"Don't you geddit? Horse of the Year. Well ridden."

"Or do you mean, Whore of the Year?" said another.

I didn't stop to think. I picked up his pint and poured it over his head.

He reached for me. I knocked his hand away, he reached for a bottle and raised it, and I hit him very hard right in the mouth. He fell over backwards and people rushed in to separate us. As the bar staff threw me out, I howled back at them all "Next time you whistle that, I'll KILL YOU."

I hadn't killed my assailant, though he did have to got to A&E for some stitches and as I lurched back to my flat, I realised that my wrist really hurt a lot. I followed on to A&E myself early the next morning, not having slept much, and they plastered up my broken wrist. "Often happens with inexperienced fighters," said the nurse. "Next time you fancy bare-knuckle boxing, keep your wrist absolutely straight in line with your arm and your fist really tight – fingers horizontal. And don't go for someone when you're drunk."

Next stop, the captain of the cricket team, hammering on my door, dismayed and infuriated to lose his opening batsman just before the start of the season.

"What are you trying to do?"

"Well - I didn't try to break my wrist," I said.

"You've ruined our chances of the area shield."

I looked at him dully. The wrist still hurt, I knew I was in for trouble with the university authorities, and suddenly, cricket didn't seem to matter. I made a snap decision I've regretted ever since.

"Sorry Gareth. But I'm giving it all up anyway. Just can't really be bothered. It's only a game."

He erupted, I told him to shut up, and eventually, to fuck off out of my room. Which he did.

A couple of days later, I was hauled before the beak – not a magistrate, just my professor, sitting with my moral tutor. I was told I was lucky to be facing them and not sitting in a courtroom charged with assault and grievous bodily harm.

I'd had enough. Of them. Of everyone. Of myself.

I managed a few pertinent phrases.

"It was self-defence."

"How can it be? You punched him in the mouth."

"Have you actually spoken to any witnesses? Have they explained that he lifted a beer-bottle with the intention of breaking it over my head?"

There was a pause. The prof looked at the tutor.

"Is that true?"

"Er, well, yes it is, but..."

The prof sighed. "You might have mentioned it."

"Gerald..." Here comes the soft soap, I thought.

"Your work is sliding. You're not the student you were. And now this. What's going on?"

I felt remote, cynical. Time to step behind my persona.

"I'm unhappy in love. It drains my life of meaning."

That shut them up for a bit.

"That sounds a little too glib...too easy..."

"Easy? It's not. You try it."

"Pull yourself together. If we have to talk to you again, you'll be suspended. Talk to people, don't lash out. And stop wasting your talent. Do some work. Go."

I sat in a grotty little cafe, nursing a vile cup of instant coffee, staring into it, reflecting. They were right, I wasn't doing much studying. I was missing lectures, late with assignments. I'd just had a close shave, could have been thrown out. Someone sat down opposite me. I looked up. It was my college bar assailant. I tensed up. He grinned.

"Shortage of bottles around here. Relax."

"I'm sorry, Keith," I said. "Those stitches must have hurt."

He shrugged. "Some girls like a scar on a bloke. Makes them look hard when they're not. And I'm not. Anyway, I've come to apologise to you. Well, to Bethan really, via you. I've spread the word. Anyone doing that whistling thing will have me to deal with as well as you."

I held up my plastered wrist. "You'll be on your own, but I'll hold your jacket. Thanks."

He laughed. "Quits?"

"Quits."

Chapter Sixteen

Bethan By The River

I realised over the following days that I badly needed a sense of direction. I was drifting. I wrote in my increasingly spasmodic diary that I'd "tried love with two remarkable women," and it hadn't worked out too well. So what should I do with myself? Really, the naive arrogance of the young me. "Tried love." As if it was a one-shot game of pinball, or a football penalty.

The direction I found was my work. I thought a lot of my professor and I wanted his approval. So I worked surprisingly hard and did surprisingly well in the end-of-year exams. I kept up my melancholic persona, enjoying the hat, long dark coat and red scarf until the weather got too warm to persist. I still needed some cover, to project a different personality from the one underneath. Psyche and I were lost to each other because of what she'd suffered and I felt I'd lost Bethan to a promiscuous round of drinking and casual sex. My own casual sex during these months didn't seem to count, of course.

It all kept going round in my head. Bethan had gone because I couldn't stay away from Psyche; now I'd lost Psyche because I did as she'd told me. I worried that she felt unclean, polluted, and so unable to be a complete lover. If so, it was my fault. I'd done as she'd told me, and left her to face her torments alone. I couldn't hack it. So I turned away from it all, got on with my studies.

One evening a month or so, after I broke my wrist on Keith's face, it was out of plaster and I was leaning on a railing looking out at the lights of Birkenhead across the Mersey. I became aware that someone had adopted a similar position a couple of feet away.

"Ça va, M'sieu Bruant? Où est le chapeau noir?"

Bethan grinned at me. I smiled back.

"Dans Le Moulin Rouge avec la plume de ma tante. Are you following me?"

"Why not? Apparently I'll follow anything in trousers."

"Oh Bethan, please don't take any notice of pissed young – "

"Loosen up, Gerry. It's okay. Look, I just wanted to thank you for stopping all that whistling. It was getting to be a real drag. And I was sorry to hear you broke your wrist."

A pause. We both looked at the dark water.

"I have been a bit of a loose woman actually, Gerry bach. I didn't know what else to do, after you. It's been rather fun," she said defiantly. "I've learned a lot."

"Are you...going steady?" A ridiculously quaint term.

"If you mean, am I screwing anyone, or am I in love? No, and also, no."

Another water-searching pause.

Eventually: "It...none of it added up to you." She was weeping quietly.

I reached over, took her hand and squeezed it. She didn't look at me.

"Are you still in love with Psyche?"

I waited, thinking hard, considering the idea as if from outside.

"And don't lie, or be kind or..."

"I think I am, yes."

She tried to pull her hand away.

"Ask me the same about you." I turned her towards me.

"I won't lie."

"Well?" Almost fiercely, glaring at me.

A tense pause. I was searching, remembering.

"I hated watching you out with other boys. I was worried when I saw you pissed outside The Crack and went to help but Eglantine waved me away, told me I was a twat."

"So you were." She managed a tense little laugh.

"So I am. Hopeless. But I never stopped loving you, Bethan, I know that now."

"I never understood that. I couldn't really be in love with two people at once. Though I can shag two people at once."

I let go of her hand. She turned away to look down at the water. "Just a kind of showing off, really. Not as much fun as people seem to think."

Not a revelation I enjoyed, but I did admire her frankness.

"It seems I can...love two people at once, I mean, and I still don't really know what to do about it." My turn to weep. "I'm just a mess. I thought time would teach me which way to turn. It didn't, I just...God, I'm so sick of myself, the inside of my head..."

She turned back to me, reached up and pulled my head down. She kissed me gently and lengthily, almost tentatively.

"Was that nice?" she said.

"Yes, really nice."

"Good. We need to talk. We may also need to screw. Come up'n see me some time. Soon." She walked slowly off. My heart was humming gently, the first time for months.

I did come up and see her. I did land up in her bed. I felt comforted and I think Bethan did too. So my second year in Liverpool ended more calmly than it started. Our relationship didn't feel the same as it used to, of course. There was something more self-contained about Bethan. I don't mean in bed, where she applied some things new to me that came from The Interregnum, as I called it.

"Are you jealous of where I learned this, cariad?"

"Hell no, let's go!"

And afterwards, we often smoked a joint. That sweet grassy smell was getting more and more common. We didn't much like the resin plus tobacco mixture, because neither of us smoked tobacco, but the dried leaves, the grass itself, that was just fine, when we could get it. And we both were drinking less.

I lurched out of my second year, studies still intact, Bethan back with me. She came down and stayed in the pub and we worked together in the bar, earning some useful money. We went up to the Marquee and the Flamingo a few times. I told myself she wouldn't enjoy the music at Scott's. More truthfully, I knew I would feel uncomfortable there, with Bethan in Psyche's realm.

We had a great evening at the Marquee with John Mayall. Clapton had moved on and I knew nothing of Peter Green. A revelation; such a lovely touch, so much melodic beauty as well as blues energy. Bethan loved it. The joint was heaving, she clung on to me and her face shone. We planned to head out with our bar cash and travel, somewhere, anywhere, but Bethan was called home. Her father was unwell.

During the time with Bethan at my home, I had stayed away from Tony and The Transition house, as well as George's Floating World. I didn't really want Bethan exposed to Tony's line on The Transition. I hated the idea that they might fall out. Bethan could be pretty direct in her opinions. However, Tony and I had some long phone conversations.

The Transitionists were back in town, most of them, but without Terry and most of The Elect. They were increasingly seen as simply part of the London Scene, featuring in "underground" press articles, getting a few radio and TV interviews and collecting a lot of hostile attention from the mainstream press. The Transition House, Tony told me without much enthusiasm, was buzzing, the coffee bar was busy, but he felt on the edge of things. He still didn't want to live at home with George, so he had moved into a little flat above his record shop, which had been reborn as a hippy centre selling records, posters, some clothes, books, incense – and drugs, if you knew how to ask.

"What?" I'd said, rather loudly.

"Just dope, Gerry, loosen up man. Though acid can be obtained if you ask nicely."

"You'll get busted, Tony."

"Possibly, but probably not. Dad and I have a good relationship with the local heat."

The other experience he was offering was a combined Tarot and Astrology session, as he had done for me, only he was charging a substantial sum for it.

"Come and see it all, Gerry, join the revolution."

"Sometime, Tony, not just now. I'm with Bethan, you see."

The line went quiet. Then:

"I've had a talk with Psyche about you. I know she sent you away."
I tensed up. "I still don't really know why. " I relaxed a little. "But I
know she would like to see you again."

"I'd like that too, Tony, when the time is right, so please give her my
love."

"Sure. Gotta split. Customers."

I put the phone back on the hook. I knew Psyche must have graduated from music school and I knew she had secured a job with the
Welsh National Opera for the autumn season. That felt good. She had
a lovely voice, and she was launched. Things seemed to be rolling along
well for her.

After Bethan left abruptly to see her parents, I worked on in the bar
for a few days. Without her, it seemed less like a warm social haven and
more like a roomful of noisy old bores. Unkind of me, but if you don't
drink and join in, you feel increasingly out of it. So you drink. That's
the barman's trap, the landlord's too.

"Have one yourself, Gerry?"

"Kind of you, but not just now, thanks."

"Good God, boy, have you taken the pledge?"

I was saved from all this by a tearful phone call from Colwyn Bay.

"Please come up. My dad's really quite ill. Mum would like it, and
I...I need you."

Bethan opened the door and threw herself at me. Mrs Jennings
hovered in the background, looking tired and strained.

"Put him down and let him in, Bethan." She managed a smile and
gave me a firm hug. "It's very good to see you again, Gerry, and thank
you." I knew she didn't just mean thanks for coming up to see them.
I looked her in the eye. "It's for me to thank you and your lovely
daughter, Mrs Jennings." Where did these pompous phrases come
from?

She had a little tear at that.

"I think you and I could manage with 'Daphne' now," she said.

The Good Doctor had had a stroke and was not at all well. He was still in hospital. They went to see him; they came back upset. I helped get a meal on the table. Daphne said, "Shall we go for a walk on the beach?" which helped. We talked about his health and the fact that he was 14 years older than Daphne, "though he is...has been...pretty fit, really. Hill walks and so on."

She looked desolate.

"I was so young and useless when we got married, I don't know what I'd do..." She turned away, walked off and watched the sea. I could see her shaking a little from sobs. Bethan and I looked helplessly at each other. She gestured towards her mother and gave me a gentle shove.

I was about the age Daphne was when she married. I felt naive and clumsy. I wandered over to her and put a hand on her arm. The usual clichés began to form and a few of them got out. "He'll pull through, he's strong ..." She didn't stop crying, looking down at the sand. I reached down for her hand and beckoned Bethan over. We walked her back home, hand in hand, and sat her down on the sofa. I poured her a brandy. Bethan sat next to her and put her head on her mother's shoulder.

Dr Jennings died the next day. I realised I didn't even know his first name.

So much to do when someone dies. The three of us took it on. Bethan was forthright and sensible with undertakers, vicars, and family members. Daphne was kind, gentle, and patient. I was dogsbody and fixer.

"I can't come to the funeral, really, I don't have a suit, and..."

Daphne grabbed my hand and squeezed it hard. "You must. Please, Gerry, I need you there, and so does Bethan."

And that was how I became a pallbearer at my first ever funeral. I learned many things about funerals, among them that women can look really foxy in black, whereas blokes often just look dowdy and embarrassed. I felt a bit furtive thinking like that about Bethan and her mother. But I told them both that they looked splendid just before we walked in with the coffin and I think that helped them onwards.

I learned that a sudden kind of sharp but temporary grief can strike, even when you hardly knew 'the deceased.' What a grotesque term. I even felt sad that I couldn't have an argument with him. And I learned that beautiful music can really crease you up, even though it does also help.

He'd known a lot of people. It felt like a long service and the house was full for an hour or two afterwards. "Thank God for the caterers," said Bethan, suddenly the accomplished hostess, then she steered me towards Someone who Mattered: "Have you met my special friend Gerald?"

"I'm sure you're a great help and comfort, Gerald," he said, winking at me. Gruesome old git.

Later on, as Daphne walked past me to talk to an ancient relative, she breathed out quietly in my direction "Oh God, will they ever go home?" I was touched by her confiding in me like that; my position in the family had changed.

We all three went to bed exhausted. I was surprised to find Daphne had made up a double bed for Bethan and me. She caught the look on my face and managed a weary smile. "It's 1966, Gerry. Times change."

I got up in the night for a pee and heard a sound downstairs. I crept down, and found Daphne sobbing her heart out at the kitchen table. She heard me, stood up and came over to me. "Daphne..." I managed before she threw her arms around me. I held her for what seemed an age, then eased her down on a chair. I sat opposite.

"I'm sorry," she gulped.

"Please don't be."

"I don't know what to do."

I watched her for a moment, and words came from somewhere.

"You'll do better than you would ever have thought possible. You have friends, you have family. You have Bethan. And I'll do what I can."

Chapter Seventeen

Settlement

T hroughout my third year, I was more like a member of the family than simply Bethan's boyfriend. We made frequent weekend visits to Daphne in Colwyn Bay and spent some of the time there catching up on our academic work; it all felt settled, and strangely virtuous.

"I feel almost married," I said to her one Monday morning on the way back to Liverpool. Bethan had bought a battered old Mini and she had passed her test first time. She didn't take her eyes off the road, she just smiled.

"Would it be such a bad thing if we were?" she asked. We left the question hanging in the air.

Dr Jennings' death had pushed me over some sort of line. I did think about Psyche occasionally and we sometimes wrote to each other, but as the months went by, she came to seem more remote, part of a distant scene, a previous life. I was anchored in Liverpool and Colwyn Bay, no longer adrift between university and George's Floating World.

My Dearest Gerry,

I thought you might like to know that I did get that job with the Welsh National. Only in the chorus, naturally, but let's hope it's just a beginning. You might also like to know that we're playing Liverpool early next year. I can get tickets for you and Bethan, if you like. Up to you, of course. But one of the works we're touring is "Così," and you used to love the trio, at least.

Would you like to give Tony a ring? George and I are a bit worried about him - just for a change! But it's not the usual thing.

George says hello and when can you come and see us again? "Soave sia il vento," gentle winds, no more stormy seas for you and me to navigate now, I think!

I was unsure of my next move. I could talk it over with Bethan, maybe even show her the letter, try for a different understanding.

"I don't like 'my dearest Gerry,' you are my dearest Gerry, not hers." My straightforward Bethan.

"It's her class, her background speaking, just a phrase. Look, if she was...angling for me, would she invite you as well as me to the opera?"

"Well, I don't really like opera..."

"Have you ever been to one?"

"...but if me being there stops you trying to get into her knickers, I'd better string along."

"She'll be on stage in costume. Long shot, Bethan."

She giggled. "Fair play. What does she mean by the final paragraph?"

"What she says. All is calm between us."

"When's the performance?"

"Later in the year some time."

Bethan paused, then did something between a "h'mm" and a "har-rumph."

She looked hard at me.

"How do you feel about her now?"

I paused.

"Well…calm. Affectionate, nothing more."

"Well don't you be getting too bloody affectionate, boyo."

I didn't find Bethan's suspicious sort of jealousy stifling, as I once did. We had settled into a confidence with each other, a growing security.

In a long phone conversation with Tony, he made clear to me his concerns over this kind of security.

"You'll bore yourselves to death, Gerry."

I got hot and bothered.

"There's nothing boring about Bethan."

"Hey, take it easy, man. It will be the whole scene of just the two of you, up close, day after day, it's not to do with her in particular."

"Maybe we like just being up close, the two of us."

"It's not the liking it that matters, it's getting rid of your contradictions and connecting to the eternal you, it's…"

"Tony, I'm not joining The Transition, so please lay off. I'm happy being Beige. I'm also okay with you being in The Transition. We just have to…differ."

Long pause.

"I miss your company, you boring little shit."

"And I miss yours, you twat."

Another pause.

"I'll stay in touch Tony, I'll try to get to see you."

But I didn't, for far too long.

Some time in 1967, I walked up to my front door and saw a familiar shape leaning against the crumbling neoclassical porch. He had on some sort of cloak. His hair was longer than I remembered it, with a scarf tied round his head.

"Tony! What the fuck are you doing here?"

"Good to see you too, Gerry." We both smiled at the echo and he gave me my second bloke hug.

"Can I stay with you for a day or two?"

I held him at arm's length and looked into his face. He seemed tense.

"Come in."

It was a shared flat and I chucked some stuff about to make a seat for him.

"Tea?"

Over tea and a joint, he explained that he was "under investigation" by The Transition. They were alarmed at his popularity and the success of his record shop as a centre for the underground scene. They accused him of mixing with political subversives and they really disapproved of his drug taking. And they were telling him to stop the astrology/Tarot "nonsense."

"It's not nonsense, is it, Gerry? You know that, don't you?" It was this tone that worried me as much as anything, this pleading for recognition. I was about to suggest he told them to take a running fuck at themselves, when Bethan walked in.

"Hello, cariad, the door was open so I...oh. Sorry. Is this profound?"

We must both have looked intense.

We stood up.

"Bethan, this is Tony, my London..."

"Oh, I know where you're from Tony, I've heard a fair bit about...about how much you mean to Gerry."

She smiled at him and he smiled back. So far, so good.

She asked Tony about The Transition and his current difficulties with them. Tony's anxiety and distress were plain.

"Ah, bechod, don't let on so, I bet you know what you really want in life, more than they do."

I was fascinated as I watched her build Tony back up in a way that would have been beyond me. I felt as though I was watching a stranger at work. She was studying psychology and social sciences and perhaps that was part of it, but it was more about her sound practical good sense. She made it very clear that The Transition wasn't for her, but it was also clear how concerned she was for his position in it. She asked lots of questions and listened closely to his answers. He told her about Honduras.

The conversation moved from the flat to the pub, via a chippy, and back to the flat.

Then Bethan really startled me. Frightened me, even.

"And how about your family, Tony? Their part in all this? What about that lovely sister I've heard so much about?"

She turned and looked steadily at me.

"A bit too much, if I'm honest, but fair play, we seem to be over that now, don't we, Gerry?"

Was I being manipulated into a statement in front of Psyche's brother? I stared at her. Or was she just being her usual direct self? They waited for my answer.

"Well, Gerry?" Tony asked quietly.

I answered as truthfully as I had that night down by the Mersey.

'I shall never stop caring deeply about Psyche; she will always be a special person to me. I think you know that, Bethan."

"Oh, indeed I do," she said.

"And I think you know what I feel for you, Bethan."

"Yes. Yes, I think I do." But she did emphasise "think" just a little.

Tony stood up.

"Look, I really didn't want to come between you two, I think I'd better go."

I wasn't having that.

"The sofa's yours, Tony. I'll get a blanket and we'll see what's what tomorrow."

Bethan said, "You should stay, Tony. It's been good to talk to you and I'm sure Gerry's pleased to see you. I've rather obstructed his London visits. He tells me regularly how he misses your company."

"You must have misheard me, Bethan, more like I missed his breakfasts and he rolls a good joint."

Tony did indeed roll a good joint. All three of us began to relax. Bethan didn't smoke much weed, and it just about put her to sleep. She went off to my bedroom and I came back to settle Tony down on the sofa.

"She's a Welsh jewel, Gerry, richer and rarer than you deserve."

"Shut up and go to sleep."

I was absurdly delighted by his good opinion.

The tickets for "Così" arrived by post, with a note in Psyche's handwriting, which said simply "See you both there, and afterwards, I hope."

Bethan was on edge about the whole outing. I was pleased we were on home territory and not at "The Garden." Opera audiences at this time were getting more mixed. There were some people in full evening dress and formal frocks, "proper toffs" as Bethan put it, and also more casually dressed younger people. We were pretty much at the scruffy end of the audience's sartorial spectrum, though Bethan looked very sexy in a tight wool dress.

"All new to me, this stuff," she said, as we dropped our tatty old coats off.

"Fun, isn't it?"

"Well, it's interesting. Where's your star of the show then?"

I recognised that her nerves were partly caused by meeting Psyche.

"Look, she's not a star, she's only in the chorus."

But she wasn't only in the chorus. A man in evening dress came on the stage as soon as the lights were down and announced, to our astonishment, that "because Miss Price is unwell, the part of Dorabella this evening will be sung by Miss Psyche Primera."

I blushed like a schoolboy, I don't know why, and joined in some light applause.

"Why are they applauding? She hasn't sung anything yet."

My heart sank. Would Bethan be hostile all evening? I thought we'd straightened this out.

"It's just a courtesy, welcoming a newcomer to the stage."

"How is she qualified to sing this? It's a big role, isn't it?" Which at least showed she'd read the programme.

"Oh for Christ's sake Bethan! She learned the role at music college and sang it in their final production. It's the Welsh National, they wouldn't put her on if they didn't think she could do it."

She fidgeted a bit, muttered "Okay, sorry," and the ludicrously unpleasant story got going. This was long before surtitles and Bethan's attention wandered, naturally.

"How's it going?" I whispered as the men onstage hatched their nasty plot in a café.

"Well, it's...okay, I guess."

When Psyche came on, Bethan's gaze locked on to her and she went very still. In the applause after the sisters' duet "Ah guarda, sorella," she turned her head and looked at me.

"She is...very beautiful."

"So are you."

That was a wrong note and we both knew it.

"No. She is beautiful."

Luckily, someone shushed us. I took Bethan's hand. She placed it on her thigh.

After the Trio "Soave sia il vento," I looked at her and saw tears in her eyes. The singing? Tension about Psyche being released? During the applause, I took her hand.

"Hell of a song, cariad," was all she said.

At the interval, we squeezed our way out to a bar and had a drink and when we got back, there was a note on my seat.

"How did that get there?" Bethan said.

The note simply said, "Bethan and Gerry, please do come to my dressing-room afterwards for a quick glass. Just show this note to one of the ushers."

"Look. Are you game?" She looked nervous and uncertain. I knew better than to force it.

The applause for Psyche was long and loud, with someone near us shouting "Bravo."

"Should be Brava," muttered Bethan.

"So - shall we go backstage?"

To my surprise, she said "Yes, of course. This is all so exciting. To meet my rival."

"Oh come on, you're..."

I realised she was winding me up and enjoying it. And at last she was allowing herself to be excited by the whole occasion.

We were both a little inhibited by Psyche's achievement, her glamour. Suddenly she was an opera star. Dorabella's wig was back on its stand and Psyche was holding a hairbrush when we came in. After we'd both told her she was fantastic as Dorabella, I gushed.

"And thank you, this is such a thrill. I've never been in a dressing room before..."

"Well, even if you have been," said Bethan, "it'd better stop right here."

Psyche laughed. "I could have him thrown out, Bethan, and we could have the champagne for ourselves."

The two women were laughing at me.

Bethan looked into Psyche's face and said, with an impulsive honesty that always melted me, "He never told me how beautiful you are. And your voice... I mean truly. I have never heard an opera before, didn't like the idea much, to be honest, but...your voice..."

Psyche reached for Bethan's hands, drew her in and kissed her on the cheek.

"And he never told me how attractive you are."

Bethan blushed.

"But listen, del, they shouldn't put you in wigs. Your hair is just wonderful."

We had a glass of champagne. Such high life! And then Psyche said, almost humbly, "We're here for three days. Can I come and see you, I wonder, during the day?"

I looked at Bethan to gauge her response but she was already saying "Oh please do."

"Psyche, this could be the making of your career, I guess."

"Oh, just a lucky break," she said. "It happens occasionally. I was fortunate that I'd sung it before."

As she sat on our battered old sofa with her long legs tucked under her, it was impossible not to look at Psyche through the sheen of her performance. She had the same grace, the same natural cool, that she'd had since I first met her. But she told us that she found life on tour quite lonely, and it hadn't helped as much as she'd thought to land a big part so early. Others in the company were envious.

"I was just in the right place at the right time. Other equally experienced mezzos in the company didn't know the part."

Maybe so, but I think all three of us knew that she had an indefinable personal quality that, along with her voice and her hard-earned technique, meant she was already a star. Being beautiful was part of it, naturally, but there was an inwardness about her that drew people to her.

That day in Liverpool, as she drank tea with us, was the start of a revelatory journey for all three of us.

"You're modest, aren't you?" objected Bethan. She made it sound like a character fault.

"Well, realistic, I hope."

"What's a mezzo-soprano, anyway?" Bethan was fascinated.

"It's more about the sort of voice. It's much the same range as soprano-soprano, but people say we have a warmer, less brilliant colour to our voices."

We chatted on about singing, opera, jazz, then Bethan said "How's your brother?"

"Gerry is a really good, loyal friend to Tony. I sometimes think he's Tony's only true friend." She paused, deciding how much to tell us.

"He's going off the deep end, I think. He's in trouble with The Transition people. You know about The Transition?"

"Oh, yes," Bethan said, fairly neutrally. "He stayed with us for a couple of days."

Psyche looked at her a moment, appraising her.

"It's his astrology and Tarot stuff. It doesn't fit with their beliefs. Also...he's taking acid. I think they may chuck him out."

Psyche looked down at the floor, her face full of sadness.

"He comes across as a rebel, ploughing his own furrow. But I think he's...lost."

Bethan charged in.

"You must go down and see him, Gerry. Soon."

Psyche and I looked at each other.

"Could you?" she said.

"Can I come too?"

Psyche and Bethan smiled at each other.

"A neutral outsider. Might do him good," said Bethan.

"You know, I think it might."

George was delighted to see us. He was courteous and kindly to Bethan, as I'd known he would be. He put us in Tony's old room.

"He's still kipping over at that gruesome shop, then?"

A weary little smile.

"Oh, yes. He does come by occasionally. He'll be very pleased to see you and he's already met you, hasn't he, Bethan?"

"Indeed he has, he dropped in on us in Liverpool," she said. "We'll go tomorrow."

Tony had a lot to tell us.

"It's the Church of the Sacramental Transition now. We have no contact with Terry. Changes filter down from on high. The inner circle, the Elect, are in Chicago."

"What circle are you in?"

"I'm outside the outer circle, Bethan, and it's lonely."

She took his hand.

"Go on. Tell us more."

"Well...there's lots of people around The Transition House but they mean nothing to me. They just think it's a part of so-called swingin' London. I keep away. I've done my job. Nehemiah is out of there. But I'm in mourning for Honduras...the revelations."

"What about the Tarot, the astrology...?"

"Oh, I dunno, Gerry, I'm trying for ways to integrate The Transition with my insights from Tarot and the stars, can't see where to go. I keep getting The Tower...is it the lighting flash of a power that will finally free me from the mundane and the mediocre? Is it an energy beyond my capacity to endure? I'm more scared than I'm prepared to let on."

He was starting to wander, his arms clutched around himself.

"I sit with The Beyond, waiting. Then I turn up the Hermit. He tells me I must carry my own light. He comes to me in dreams. Once, on a trip, he merged into me and my head was resounding with creaks and groans like wood under pressure, then a splintering crack and I was staring at the night sky but...as usual...no stars just clouds and dull light, light that pulsed and then faded."

He was staring at the table, leaning forward, head bowed. Bethan and I looked at each other over his back. She asked "Tony, please don't think I disapprove, but...do you really think the acid trips are helping?"

He sat back, unwound his arms and took Bethan's hand. He smiled at her, looking at her. I think he was reckoning up the gap between his experience of life and hers.

"Thing is, Bethan, early trips were blessings. A new relationship with the immediate world. I could stare at a sunlit corner of the shop and it was a world of beauty and meaning that included me. It's not usually like that now. Gerry, you once said to me something by some poet, that the world is too much with us..."

He tailed off and I completed it: "...late and soon, getting and spending, we lay waste our powers. Little we see in Nature that is ours; we have given our hearts away, a sordid boon."

Tony gave a little snort.

"A sordid boon. The shop's doing so well, people pay me a lot to go out there and explore their psyche but do I see much in nature that is mine? What does that mean? You two seem so happy with each other and I'm really pleased about that. But I thought Honduras would be a final answer, a total resolution... can there be such a total thing anyway? I have to get away from The Beige but my Transition is somewhere else now. Getting stoned sometimes calms my view, taking acid can still be ecstatic. I move amongst people all the time, talking, thinking, acting, so why am I so fucking LONELY?"

He sounded desperate.

We spent most of a couple of days with him. It may have helped him; his mood swings were getting wilder, but he was very pleased when I asked him to be my best man.

It nearly didn't happen. One night I was sitting up in bed waiting for Bethan. When she came out of the bathroom, she said "hang on," and listened. "Something's up with Psyche," and she disappeared into her room.

I sat there dozing, until I heard voices raised in pain and dismay. The door swung open and Bethan came hurrying over to me. Her face was closed and angry.

"That poor woman, why didn't you tell me, you..." and she slapped me hard round the face. "You did sleep with her, or you would have done, if..." and she burst into tears and ran back to Psyche.

They both came into the room and sat on the bed. My face still stung. I didn't say anything, just looked at them as they held each other. Eventually Psyche said, "I'm going to bed. Goodnight. Thank you, Bethan. I've never told anyone else so..."

"Not a word, never."

Big hugs, and off she went.

"Did that hurt?

"Of course it did."

"Good."

"Fuck off, Bethan. I didn't lie to – "

"Depends on what you mean by 'slept with,' doesn't it?"

"What I mean is...I mean, I never hid from you what I felt about Psyche."

"And now?"

"Oh go to sleep."

Psyche was standing in the doorway, tears running down her face.

"Please. Please...just...don't..."

Bethan walked over to her, and led her back into her room like a child.

I didn't, and still don't, quite understand my rage. I called after Bethan.

"Hey, why don't you marry Psyche instead? You seem to be closer to her than..."

But Psyche's cry of pain silenced me.

I didn't sleep well.

After that night, the two women I loved were welded together like the closest of sisters. After that night, my relationship with Bethan was changed. We patched things up. She used to go and see Psyche on her own from time to time and they had long phone conversations. I knew next to nothing of those conversations. When I tried to ask, I was firmly shut out, by both of them.

"I'm grateful to you, Gerry, for bringing Bethan to me, really I am. I'm only sorry if what I told her that night has damaged your relationship, but..."

"Well, maybe...changed, more than damaged. I dunno. Maybe no bad thing."

"I've never had such a close and trustworthy female friend."

Marriage didn't get an especially good press around this time, among my friends at least. From the left wing of my acquaintance, because it was seen as "a bourgeois festival of sexual expropriation." More generally, because of the loosening of moral restraints and religious convictions around the whole business. What was the big deal about virginity, anyway? I don't remember much discussion about children and the importance of a stable relationship around them. I do remember Bethan saying, as we discussed marriage, that it seemed a lot less important if you weren't thinking about having children.

"Nevertheless," she said in her forthright way, "if you are asking me to marry you, despite not kneeling in front of me with a bloody great diamond ring, for which I will forgive you: yes. About time!"

It was a pretty ordinary room, with a row of artificial flowers in front of the desk, a few rows of seats, a beige carpet. Tony would be grinning at that, I thought, and when I turned in his direction, that's exactly what he was doing.

"Nice carpet," he murmured. "Very suitable."

"You just concentrate on not dropping the ring, d'Artagnan." He was wearing his sinister-looking cloak. "You're bloody lucky to be here at all."

It felt as though we were waiting around in an airport lounge but then, we'd been firm about not going to a church. "Wouldn't be right, just to use it when it suits us," Bethan said to my parents. Daphne had given me a great big hug when I said we were getting married and started crying when I asked if that would be okay with her. So there we were, in the registrar's domain.

In she came, with her assistant. A bit of a bustle-bottom, bossing us around in a benevolent fashion. She did the preliminaries, and then we were off. No "Wedding March," just a tape of "With a Little Help From My Friends," and in came Bethan. It was raining outside and she'd got her hair a bit wet, which troubled her; I thought it was appealingly natural.

There was a lot of good feeling in the room. We had friends and family present but, without the church-type ritual, there was a bit of a vacuum. This was long before "celebrants" and home-designed ceremonies. The actual ceremony was feeling rather flat.

That is, until the registrar said "you may kiss the bride." How kind of her to give us permission, I thought grumpily, but Bethan, as I bent to kiss her, said "little surprise for you, cariad." As we touched lips, a beautiful voice swept over us all from the back of the room. I knew at once it was Psyche, unaccompanied, singing a lovely aria. Bethan's face was shining; we held each other tight until the song finished. We were all a little stunned and the ensuing silence simply wouldn't do, so I turned round and started clapping. Tony leapt to his feet and applauded, and so did everyone else. Someone shouted "encore," but Psyche had already slipped out the back.

Afterwards, whilst our friends got pissed in short order, I was able to thank Psyche properly. "Just wonderful. Perfect wedding present."

"I'm so pleased you liked it, Gerry. Actually, I was terrified, much harder than an opera house. Bethan's idea. Do you know the song? It's Mozart, from Figaro, 'Voi, che sapete,' you women who know what love is. And she does, you know, your Bethan."

I looked at her. "And so do you. And so do I. I feel so lucky I could burst."

"Bit messy on your wedding day, Gerry," said Bethan behind me. She reached up, hugged Psyche and kissed her on the cheek. Tony appeared out of nowhere and swept all of us into his cloak for a big hug, then swung away, cloak swirling magnificently, to pay attention to the young woman serving drinks at the bar.

Psyche watched him.

"He seems much happier today, calmer," said Bethan.

Without taking her eyes off him, Psyche said "So it seems... I'm not sure, maybe it's just the positive vibe flowing around here. He may slump later…look," turning back to us, "I'm sorry. It's your wedding day, not my family therapy day."

"After that song, you can do whatever you want," I said.

"How about a drink?"

Chapter Eighteen

Expulsion and Flight

Married life was good. No more hitch-hiking. M. Bruant's black hat was on a shelf in the bedroom. I was studying in London, at the School of Oriental and African Studies, working on a Masters, learning Arabic, studying hard. Bethan was doing teacher training. We saw Psyche, when she was in town, and Tony occasionally, but we moved in different circles, as you might say if you wanted to excuse yourself. Or as he put it, "You're going straight. And straighter. Beigebeigebeige ..."

We had a ropey little flat somewhere near the Angel tube station. Late one evening, there was a hammering on the door. I opened it and Tony almost fell into the room.

"They've thrown me out," he cried, and burst into tears.

We helped him down on to our sofa bed, Bethan held his hand and we applied tea and marijuana therapy. He looked awful. Grey face, eyes flicking round the room, long hair stringy and greasy.

When he was a little calmer, I asked him why it mattered so much. He had his own scene and a good little business.

"I've no direction. You can't know what it feels like. It's getting harder and harder to reach The Beyond. My shrink, he's good, but he doesn't really get it."

"Are you on medication?" asked Bethan.

"Yes. And he says I mustn't take acid, though a little dope is okay," he said, reaching for the spliff with a tight grin. He inhaled deeply, held it briefly and let it out slowly.

"I don't know who I am, half the time," exhaled with the smoke.

"Tony, we know who you are," said Bethan. "Your sister knows who you are. I'm sure your father knows who you are. Stop it."

"You are so much more than The Transition dogma," I added. "And anyway, why did they throw you out?"

"Same stuff I told you about. Astrology and the Tarot. And... and drugs. They are scared of acid."

Not just them, I thought, but said nothing. I knew he'd taken a lot of it.

"Are you still meditating?"

"Yes. But... I can't... I can't get THROUGH. The gate. It's shut. It's fucking SHUT in my face. He...Terry...he shut me out. I KNOW he did."

He bent over in tears and put his face on his knees.

Bethan and I looked at each other helplessly. I hated myself for thinking it, just when Tony needed us, but all the time in the background was the nagging worry that Bethan had a class the next morning and I had an Arabic test. And Tony was talking crazed metaphysical processes that really existed only in his own mind.

We needn't have worried. The sobs gradually subsided, until Bethan said softly, "He's gone to sleep."

We helped him on to the sofa and took his shoes off. Bethan wrinkled her nose; he was not very fragrant. We settled him as comfortably as we could. He stirred a little but slumbered on.

We sat watching him for a while, then we went to bed, where we sat up worrying together.

"He's undernourished, exhausted and unwell. What can we do with him? For him?"

"I don't know. He's my oldest friend and I don't know what would help him. This fucking cult has taken him somewhere I can't follow. I...just don't know..."

I was getting upset. Beth held me and said, "You know, face it. There may be nothing you or anyone can do, other than the shrinks."

We slept uneasily. How crazy was Tony? Would he do something mad in the night? I realised I knew almost nothing about mental illness but, luckily, Bethan was better informed.

I'd heard Tony go to the toilet in the night but when we got up he was more or less as we'd left him. He muttered and mumbled and thrashed around a bit, while we gulped down some breakfast. Just as we were getting ready to go, he sat up.

"Where are you going? Don't leave me. Please."

"Tony, we have to go out. I can come back at lunchtime and Bethan'll be back around 4 or 4:30. Have something to eat. Help yourself. Have a shower. Just stay put, this is your sanctuary."

He stared at me and sat up. "You too, you're deserting me, like the rest."

"Three and a half hours, Tony, that's all. Eat, have some tea, smoke a joint, read a book, listen to some grooves. I promise we'll come back to you in a bit. I promise."

"OK, man." He sat back. "Don't desert me, is all."

"We won't, if you don't talk like a twat."

He managed a taut grin. "OK then, fuck off."

So we did.

When I got back to the flat, soon after two, there was a note: "Thanks. Haven't slept so well in months. I'm off to Chicago. Thanks for the nutrients." He'd eaten most of the food in our fridge.

Chicago?

I rang the flat. George answered. He hadn't seen Tony for weeks. When he tried to get to him in the shop, Tony was impatient, told George he was fine, clearly didn't want him there amongst "his varied clientele," as George put it dryly. He didn't know anything about The Transition in Chicago. All I knew was that it was a kind of HQ for their operation in America and that was probably where Terry and the Elect were.

"So Chicago is not another Caribbean thing?"

"No, George, I think he's going to plead with the inner circle to let him back in."

A long sigh. "Here's hoping he fails, Gerry."

I had a "well, yes and no" sort of conversation with him on what re-entry might do to Tony, or what sort of shape final expulsion might leave him in.

"What does Psyche think?" I asked him.

"I don't know, I don't think she knows about Chicago. She's in Paris at a master class. Give her a ring in a few days, she'll be back here for a while I think."

"You know, he's quite ill," said Psyche as she sat on the sofa where her brother had slept the previous week. "He's on strong medication. I managed to get that out of him. George is paying for a clinical psychologist. Who is concerned..." she inhaled sharply "concerned he may be heading towards schizophrenia." She gave in, and wept. Bethan and I sat each side of her, holding her as she sobbed.

When she calmed, she said, "What can I do? Should I chuck my commitments and go over there?" She looked at me. "Should you?"

I didn't know what to say.

Bethan did.

"Do you really think you'd divert him, get him back? What about the damage to your career? And to Gerry's studies? He's got an interview next week for the civil service."

"No, I can't go, of course I can't, and neither must you." She looked at the floor. "But I don't know what to do."

"Can he... I mean I guess he can... get treatment over there?"

"Yes he can, his shrink gave him a Chicago contact. He told me when he phoned me from the airport."

She managed a smile. "Irresponsible brat!"

We went out for a drink and a meal. She told us about Paris and how she was working to build her career. We talked about Bethan's teaching, my upcoming interview. We all felt a sense of foreboding. I don't think that's hindsight. That evening Tony was meeting Terry in Chicago.

The journey was nightmarish; like a bad trip, Tony said later. He knew he shouldn't try to bring any illegal drugs with him, so the temporary calm of a joint was out of reach. He had enough explaining to do at O'Hare security about his anti-psychotics.

Terry sat waiting for him. London had alerted him and one of his people was keeping an eye on the airport. There was a gentle knock on the door and Johnny Walker put his head round the door. "The ex-Brother Nehemiah's here, Master Terry."

He sighed. "Send him in."

Tony looked even worse than he'd expected. He indicated a chair and sat opposite him. Tony looked round. Lurid posters, huge floor cushions, low lights. He looked at Terry. Calm, composed as ever, neatly and quietly dressed. Could work at a bank, he thought.

"Nehemiah as was. What are you doing here? What have you come here for?"

At once, he felt Terry's power over him still. He needed space, time, quiet.

"Can we meditate together? Then I might be able to find a good answer to your question."

Terry looked steadily at him.

"Tony," his use of his ordinary, Beige name made his heart sink, "of course not. You are no longer a Transitionist. We have moved on. We are holding Unburdenings on the streets of Chicago, New York, Miami, and as you will know, London. You will have to Unburden and study and submit to group sessions, before you stand any chance of serving the Church of the Sacramental Transition."

Tears sprang to Tony's eyes.

"Let me back in. Please. I don't know who I am any more, without your guidance and...I truly don't know why I am here or anywhere, I..." he tailed off.

Terry kept looking at him steadily.

"When did you last take a narcotic substance?"

He never could help telling Terry the truth and he never knew why he did so. "Three days ago."

"Thank you for being truthful. Do you have any drugs on you now?"

"Only my medicines. Anti-psychotics."

"You know that we cannot have any drugs, medicines or otherwise, in The Transition House now."

"But they are prescription medicines, even the goons at the airport let me keep them and..."

"Give them to me now, or go."

He went. Shaking and red in the face with suppressed rage, he hurried past Johnny Walker on the stairs, then he turned back.

"Johnny, can I stay with you a couple of nights. Please?"

"Do you want to read my stars, sell me some drugs? You need to go home, Tony, it's no use."

"The Transition is my home and the door's slammed in my face...FUCK YOU ALL," he yelled suddenly.

Tony never knew where he slept the next couple of nights. He tried to contact the Chicago shrink. She was on holiday. Shaking and rambling, he landed up with a dealer in a bar and dropped some acid. Wandering along a town-centre street not far from Terry's HQ, the next day or the day after that, he came across people in the long dark cloaks of The Transition. They were calling out, falling to their knees. Some bystanders joined them on the pavement.

"I thought there was no God, and..."

"The Transition is coming, Brother Jehu, is it not?"

"Have you transgressed?"

"Yes, Yes, I must Unburden, I have had impure thoughts and..."

"And I smoked some dope and it made me sick."

"Unburden! Unburden!" yelled the cloaked kneelers.

Tony found himself amongst them. The pavement felt cold and hard under his knees, but he was pleased it hurt. The pain would show that he was sorry. But his Unburdening went badly wrong.

"I am Nehemiah, I have built the New Temple. You must join it. But listen. I have taken drugs and sold them and I read the Tarot. So what? SO WHAT? They won't let me back in, the fuckers. Listen. Do you know he sets up orgies for his followers? Sits and watches. Cold light in his eyes. And all the money, the cash these SUCKERS" he waved a hand round the rapidly-growing crowd "give to him, every time they sell you one of their newspapers, it all goes to HIM."

He was on his feet now, swaying and shouting, tears running down his face, gulping for breath.

"Who am I? They won't tell me. Nehemiah, my arse. Look. I served them. And now they won't let me in. They...not these in front of you, not the poor bloody sore knees, no, the Elite, his inner circle, the spiritual Nazis of the New Sacrament, they..." he didn't see the cop coming, swinging his nightstick, but Johnny Walker did and headed him off. They had a brief conversation, and the cop stood back to watch.

Johnny and another cloaked figure came each side of Tony, grabbed his arms and marched him quickly backwards until he staggered off-balance, then they dragged him to a cab, shoved him in, got in one each side and one of them hit him hard.

"Shut the fuck up, traitor."

He passed out.

When he came to, his head hurt. Blood was drying on his face. He lay on a mattress on the floor, in a small, dark room with a rectangle of window above head-height. He rolled over with a groan and saw there was a toilet in the corner. Christ, it's their very own prison cell, he thought. His hands were shaking.

He went to the door and banged on it. No response. He banged again and went back to sit on the mattress. The door opened and Johnny Walker came in. Before Tony could say anything, Johnny launched into apologies and justifications. He was sorry Brother Lazarus had hit him, that wasn't necessary. He hoped Tony understood that The Church of the Sacramental Transition couldn't accept him disrupting their public rituals.

"Look, Terry can't take you back in. It's not just the drugs, it's the superstitious stuff around astrology and the Tarot. I'm really sorry about that and...what's the matter?"

Tony was frantically checking his pockets.

"My pills. Medication. Not drug drugs."

"We've got them safe, you can have them back when you leave. We can't have any drugs of any sort in The Transition House.

"I want to leave now. NOW."

"First, you have to swear that you will never disrupt our sacred work. That you will leave Chicago and go home. And you must never attempt to contact us or rejoin us."

They were scared of him, he realised.

A tense silence grew between them. Johnny watched him as he tried to hold together his churning rage. He failed.

"Why the FUCK would I want to rejoin you? You kidnapped me, beat me up. Imprisoned me. Your...your bastard quasi-religion has stolen my personality, I don't know who I am, you... what are you grinning about?"

Johnny stood serene behind the shield of his beliefs, and smiled down at his old friend. "Acid stole your personality, Tony. We tried to save it."

A voice burst into Tony's mind. Be a soldier. Be a soldier.

He leaped up at Johnny, swinging wildly. Johnny ducked under his fists and fled. The door crashed shut.

Through the peephole: "We'll bring you some food when you calm down."

Howling and screaming didn't achieve much but it did tire Tony out so that he could sleep. When he woke, there was a tray of food by the mattress. He ate. He stared at the door. His head was full of voices.

"My head is full of voices," he said out loud. He shook his head a few times but they didn't stop. He began to sob. One voice emerged most clearly.

"Be a soldier."

"But I'm not," he said out loud.

"Be a soldier. Be a soldier. Now."

He stood in thought, walked to the door and started to hammer on it. Then he stood with his back to the wall next to the door. When it opened, he flung himself round into the doorway, bowled Johnny over and ran down a corridor. Johnny pounded after him, yelling, "Wait! Tony! I've got your pills, and your wallet and passport and things."

Tony stopped, turned round and stared at Johnny as he caught up with him.

"Give them to me."

"Come to the front desk," said Johnny. Tony grabbed his arm, spun him round and rammed his arm up behind his back, forcing Johnny to his knees. "Where are they?"

Johnny cried out in pain.

"In my pocket. Here."

He fumbled at his pocket.

"I can't get at them."

Tony hauled him to his feet and pushed him face to the wall.

"Now. Hand over." He twisted Johnny's arm a little more.

Johnny squealed, fumbled in his pocket, pulled out a wallet and passport and dropped them on the floor. As Tony bent to pick them up, Johnny swung a kick at him, missed and stumbled. Tony pushed him over and was gone, up some stairs, into a busy entrance lobby.

"Stop him!" he heard Johnny call out behind him, and someone in a cloak tried to grab his arm. Tony hit out at a face and people backed away. He barged through double doors and he was on the street, into a cab. "Airport. Please."

He phased in and out of reality. Voices were joined by hallucinations; he tried to chat to the person next to him on the plane. "You're not making a lot of sense, young man," the woman said and turned away in her seat.

"No sense. Nonsense. A lot of sense," he answered, and slept.

Chapter Nineteen

Unsettlement

Psyche, most unexpectedly for one so cool and apparently remote, had built up a TV career as host on a weekly music, chat and sketches show on BBC2. Maybe it was her cool that underwrote her success. She left the chatting up of guests to others, unless they were musicians. She had jazzers on the show, opera stars, particular kinds of comic, and it was going very well. Visiting bands would drop by en route to their tours: Art Blakey, Ben Webster and, of course, Bill Evans; string quartets, Flamenco guitarists, and once, George Harrison.

"Swinging Psyche chats up George," wittered The Sun. The camera loved her and she knew what she was talking about, so her musical guests talked well with her. When her singing career took her away from the studios for a few weeks, her temporary replacement was bright and quick-witted but it wasn't the same. Psyche's on-screen presence was loved by many people.

Bethan taught and I worked at the Foreign Office. George's family all thought I was a spy and I couldn't persuade them otherwise for years. Eventually, I said, "You know the Smiley novels? John Le Carré? Alec Guinness on TV? Yes, well I'm not George Smiley. I'm certainly not Peter Gwilliam. I'm more like an economy version of Lacon, a go-between at a lower level."

"Of course, Gerry, and that's why you can speak Arabic fluently and visit the Middle East from time to time."

"Maybe I just like it there?"

I was fascinated by the world of the secret services but I worked alongside them, not in them. I enjoyed my work; dealing with the interface between politicians and spies was not easy, but it was never boring. I had to be careful about the spy thing. Tony was calmer than he'd been in Chicago since George found the right shrink for him but he had paranoid spells and he could have easily taken hold of the idea.

Bethan and I grew steadily more prosperous. She was good at teaching and she was a primary headteacher quite early in her career. Our flat was pleasant to be in, despite the dubious attractions of 1970s Clapham. We were, I felt, pretty well settled. We wanted to start a family.

Nothing happened. For years. We had tests. Turns out it was me. My little wrigglers were not up to the job. I felt miserable about that, miserable that somehow I was letting Bethan down.

"Of course you're not letting me down," she snapped. She was working hard and the tension around not conceiving was telling on her. She reminded me, at one point in a fraught evening, that she'd always said she couldn't see the point in marriage unless you had children.

"I think what you said was 'unless you wanted children.' Not the same th..."

"Stop being such a fucking PEDANT!" Door slam, tears, reconciliation, lovemaking.

"I'm sorry I can't be a father to your children."

"It's not about you, it's about us."

It eventually turned out to be not about me but another, someone who could have children with her. IVF had hardly started in this country. It was uncertain and expensive. Jed, from Liverpool days, was not at all uncertain and he cost nothing. Or everything.

Bethan and I had pretty much let go of having sex. We'd been through a sweaty, frantic time: as much sex as we could fit in during the working week, long mornings in bed at the weekends, early nights with wine and good music. All the clichés, no results. Bethan wanted a baby so much and knew so clearly that she couldn't with me. We'd been through "but we still love each other, don't we?" Yes, but. We were affectionate, mostly we didn't argue much, we furthered our careers, we cared about each other, but we didn't go at it any more.

"Pregnant? What? How...I mean..."

"Usual method."

My spirits slumped; their underpinnings were giving way.

"We haven't been near each other for a good few weeks."

"Well quite. I thought you'd be pleased..."

"Well I would have been if I'd done it, but..."

"...for ME," she suddenly yelled, her face red, "pleased for me," and burst into tears.

I stared at her. Who was this animal? I wasn't ready to hold her yet.

"Who?"

"Who do you think?"

My turn to get cross. Didn't stop me being pompous.

"I think you owe it to me not to play paternity quiz games."

She looked at the floor, her face hot and miserable.

"Jed. You used to accuse me of being sweet on him."

"Bit more than sweet, it seems."

I became aware that I was panting, with my mouth slightly open.

"I'm not a tart, Gerry. I just want children so MUCH..."

At the time, I felt desperate and bitter. I understand rather better now that we truly are animals. Our reproductive drives are illogical, very powerful, and not necessarily in the best interests of the whole organism. Bethan was a successful career-woman but that felt incomplete. Her strategy for completion couldn't involve me. At least, not in its early stages.

At first, she wanted us to be a family together.

"We can raise the child as our own, as though you were its biological father."

"I'll have to think about that."

"Well, of course." She looked glum and uncertain.

I'd just got round to thinking that could be okay, could be fine, when I saw Bethan and Jed in a restaurant, so happy, so together, so right. Then she decided she needed to talk it all through with him again and she didn't come home that night, and then...

But this isn't supposed to be just my life story. You can fill in the rest. Down the years, I saw Bethan and her two boys occasionally. I was Uncle Gerry, one of those benevolent outsiders, a family friend who isn't really an uncle at all. I saw little enough of Jed. He always looked embarrassed, and I couldn't be dealing with that. It was his problem, a small enough price to pay for having won someone like Bethan. I never failed to admire her, and never entirely lost my love for her. Her boys were eventually told that I was their mother's first husband and I saw a bit more of them for a while. We were good friends. I just wish...well, what's the point.

When Bethan was a grandmother and seriously ill, I went to see her more than once. Her hair was grey, her face thin and strained, but she was still my Bethan. Years before, Jed had pissed off with someone else. "He only looked at life through the end of his cock," I snarled.

"Well really, I think that was all I wanted from him, at the time."
She sniggered. "Now shut up and hold me."

She sent me a note. I can't write it all out, I'll get upset and I've a
job to complete. The note was full of thankyous. She asked me to keep
an eye out for her boys, told me not to punch Jed if I saw him again.
"You'll only break your wrist." She ended: "When we were good, we
were the best. Never forget Greece. Go and see Psyche."

I must now reel back some decades so that I can finish my task. One
evening, a few years after the Chicago breakdown, Tony was having
a settled spell He was sitting with Psyche, George and me in the flat
chatting over a bottle of red when the front door intercom buzzer
went off. The metallic, distorted voice said "Domino Pizzas for you,
let me in please."

Tony was at the phone. "I didn't order a pizza, did anyone? No, I
think you've got the wrong address," but the intercom had clicked off.
George went on talking. There was a hammering on the door, and he
went quiet. I watched his face. He looked puzzled, maybe worse than
puzzled. Tony stood up. "Dad, what the – " There was a tremendous
splintering crash and the door burst open. A man stood there wearing
a mask. George leaped up. "Psyche, on the floor. Tony – " He didn't
finish the sentence.

The sound of gunfire in the room was utterly terrifying and impossibly loud. It dazed and confused us. After he had executed George,
the gunman pointed the gun at Tony, strode over to him and yelled,
"You're coming with me. Show me the safe." Tony, shaking and grey
with shock, glared at him and didn't move. He said quietly, "I don't
know where it is. Go and fuck yourself, you murderous piece of shit."

The gunman pointed the gun at Tony's face. "You're dead too," said
the gunman. He paused. "Or her," and swung the gun round towards
where Psyche lay huddled on the floor. Tony grabbed our half-full

wine bottle off the table and smacked it into the side of the man's head. He collapsed and Tony followed him down. I saw the bottle rising and falling again and again.

My ears were ringing and buzzing but there was another almost continuous sound. I realised it was Psyche screaming. I went round behind the sofa and helped her up. She turned away and vomited. In shock, trivial thoughts will pop up: what a mess, and George doesn't have a cleaner.

Tony was kneeling beside the gunman. "I've killed him," he said in a low monotone. "Just as well," I said, trembling uncontrollably, "or he'd have killed you."

To my astonishment, I took control. "We must all go into your bedroom, Tony. There may be more of them. Come ON!"

From there, with furniture shoved against the door, we phoned 999. My fingers were shaking so much I could hardly dial.

The police were difficult with Tony at first. They didn't get far.

"Why did you go on hitting him? You could have stopped after the first blow."

Tony stared at him. "When you came in and saw his body, what did you notice? I mean, what was in his hand?"

"A pistol."

"And how many times had he shot my father?"

"Looks like three or four times."

"Do you have any more questions?"

"We'll need to talk to all three of you again."

"Of course," I said, "come on Tony, he's only doing his job."

We stood outside the police station, with the blood of George and his murderer on our clothes. Tony, in particular, was horribly spattered.

"I can't go back in there yet," he said. Psyche shook her head. Little bursts of trembling took her over.

"I'll go in there and collect some stuff. Tell me what you want." I didn't know where this competent manager of disaster came from but he was proving useful. He was, however, unnerved at the thought of entering the flat. Luckily the police were still there and the bodies had gone.

We landed up at the flat of a very kindly aunt of theirs. I handed over my command to her gratefully. We washed, showered, scrubbed. She hugged us, made us hot drinks and something to eat, and fussed round in a way that was simultaneously a little irritating and very comforting. The three of us slept in her living room, Psyche in my arms. We dozed and woke up, weeping and shaking. Gradually, the sobs subsided.

I woke up with a jolt, gasping as the images came flooding back. I realised I had to phone Bethan and my parents, although it was still early. It would be in all the papers.

The Crown considered prosecuting Tony for killing his father's murderer but gave up the idea after collecting written statements from Psyche and me. Not only could it be seen to be self-defence but in fact he had probably saved all our lives, since none of us knew where George's safe was.

"I'm buggered if I know what they were thinking of," one senior policeman said quietly to me, "you'd never get a jury to convict in these circumstances."

The police worked quickly and effectively despite this being the 1970s, often seen as a nadir of British policing. The contents of the murderer's pockets gave them useful evidence and the investigation soon burst out of the courtroom and into the press, onto the radio and the TV.

Have you ever been in court? If so, you'll know the trying mixture of tension and boredom generated by criminal proceedings. Inside the odd rituals and tedious quibbles about objections and evidence, there are stories that must be told, listened to and assessed.

By the time of the trial, Tony was in a bad way. His outrageous courage during his father's murder had cost him dear and he couldn't face the courtroom for long. On the basis of his psychiatrist's statement, the judge excused Tony after he'd given evidence and he sat in a little side-room, on call, muttering to himself and turning over Tarot cards. It would have been amusing had it not been tragic.

Bethan and I sat in court each side of Psyche, holding her hands as it became clear that George had been murdered by "business rivals." The business was drug dealing at a high level.

I sat there wondering why it hadn't occurred to me. George's frequent absences, the travel, the skilfully avoided questions. The murder had been organised by a group of people, three of whom were on trial. One was "Uncle" Billy, and when he was cross-examined, Psyche had to leave the court-room, and sat outside on call, fighting for self-control.

In effect, it had been a gangland execution, because George had been trying to break free of his accomplices. He owed them money and that's why his killer demanded to know where the safe was. "Uncle" Billy received a long sentence for setting up the murder. I would have preferred a death sentence, carried out very, very slowly.

There was a media explosion. Tony vanished into the flat above his shop, which he closed. Psyche spent a lot of time with Bethan and I spent a lot of time chasing reporters away. It quickly became yesterday's story. Psyche was suffering and couldn't turn up at the BBC for her show. Eventually her contract was terminated and she was paid off. Her singing career was on hold, but that turned out to be easier for her to pick up again than the TV show.

I didn't really keep up with her career when it restarted. I saw her infrequently. Part of my distance may have been because the terrible evening of George's murder came roaring back into our minds when we saw each other. Anyway, she was often away from London, especially in Belgium, the Netherlands and the USA. The critics loved her singing. They said she was best suited to the eighteenth century and earlier, oratorios and recitals, not the big romantic roles. "Too cool for Puccini," I thought.

One morning, three years after the trial, I opened an unexpected note from her.

"Here's a ticket for Dido. Please come and see it. I think you'll like it. Come and say hello afterwards, I'll tell them to let you through backstage. There won't be hordes!" I stared at the ticket, and my head seethed with memories and questions.

It was a small company, a special London run of a production that had done well in the North. The company had hired Psyche for London, to the fury of the displaced singer and, according to the "Evening Standard," the disapproval of some of the company. It was the first night in London she'd invited me to.

I had to sit through a one-act opera first, because "Dido and Aeneas" is very short. I was so filled with restless anticipation I took very little notice of it. Psyche wasn't in it. I just wanted it gone. I liked the production of "Dido" at once. It wasn't embarrassingly updated, it didn't strain after parallels or symbols, it had no neat little extra ideas. The cast wore simple elegant clothes, the witches were suitably terrifying and the stage was mostly pretty bare. I hadn't known Purcell's music before, but it grew on me rapidly as the evening progressed. Psyche seemed to draw the audience in to her, by doing very little in the way of overt acting. Her voice was…I don't know. Richer? Deeper? Darker? Perhaps just more mature.

Then came the moment I was unprepared for, her final aria. She came on in dark trousers, a white top, and a small gold chain around her neck. She was holding what looked like a small sceptre, also gold.

It was not a large theatre and I was not far from the front of the stalls. "When I am laid in earth…Remember me, but ah! Forget my fate." She stood downstage centre, her face as pale as always, her eyes seemed huge, her dark hair was loose down her back. The tears ran down my face. In this I wasn't alone, but as the aria moved to its climax, she turned her head slightly and looked right at me.

The sceptre was a dagger. She crumpled to the floor. I almost cried out. As the opera ended and the applause rang out, I knew I'd seen a truly great performance. There was nothing histrionic or self-conscious about what we'd just seen. It was overwhelmingly, unbearably true. The audience were on their feet and wouldn't let her go, but I didn't share their elation. Psyche stood there looking drained, and then relieved when the rest of the cast joined her for a lot of bowing. I wiped my eyes and eased myself through the crowd.

I reached the dressing room before she did and stood in the middle of the floor feeling a bit silly. Then she hurried in, stopped short and just looked at me, stared at me almost blankly. I shook my head and started weeping again.

"Oh, Psyche."

She came slowly over to me, put both arms round me and hugged me hard and long. Finally, she stood back and watched my face.

"It was as though you actually meant it…I mean, you, Psyche, meant…the final aria."

She just nodded, slowly.

"Thank you for coming. I was afraid you might not want to bother with it."

"Bother? With you? My Psyche, my spirit ... I shall always be able to say I saw the first night of Psyche Palmera's Dido. It's... like saying I saw Bill Evans at Ronnie's..." I tailed off, feeling silly. I turned away and blew my nose.

"Really? Oh, thank you. You mean it, don't you...don't you?"

"I've never heard anything so beautifully sad, so all-enveloping, so..."

We stared at each other. She began to smile a little. Although the pain had faded, it was still there. I tried to lighten it.

"You'll need to go and get pissed with everyone, won't you?"

She shuddered, and startled me with "Not fucking likely. The cast don't like me much. She was very good, but what was I supposed to do? Turn it down?"

"That was before tonight. They will love you now! You were born to sing Dido."

A long pause. Then, quietly, "Yes. You're right. I think I was."

We looked at each other some more, until I felt awkward. My old desire for her was sweeping through me and I think she sensed it, though she seemed composed and calm. "Gerry," she said, "I'm going to meet a couple of people in the throng. It must be done. Then I'm going to clear off and sleep. I feel done for."

"Can't think why! I'm knackered, just watching it. I'll ring you? What number?"

She gave me her card, hugged me briefly and we left, she to after-show hurrahs, me to the Tube. I still had a dull ache but also that huge, expanded, free feeling you get when something has moved you very deeply. I thought about our conversation. She was born to sing Dido.

The reviews were adulatory. She had risen from the ranks of competent opera singers who could be sure of a second- level sort of casting, to the top of the heap for work in her style. The Telegraph wrote, "In one performance, she has identified herself as the greatest baroque and classical voice of her generation."

And, I thought, the loneliest.

Chapter Twenty

After Dido

It was some months after Dido. I hadn't seen Psyche since that evening. Tony was being treated in a psychiatric hospital and I'd only seen him twice. They were unhappy experiences for both of us. Long cream and green painted corridors, then a little room, and there was Tony standing looking out of the window.

"Gerry. What do you want? Why are you here?"

"I'm here to see my oldest friend, to see how he is."

He walked over to a chair. He seemed slow and his answers didn't connect up too well.

"Did someone send you?"

"No, of course not."

"Of course." He looked up at me with little interest.

"It's like Dallinghoo, the food. Shite, really. But they're quite nice. I guess."

He meant the staff.

"What do you do with your time?"

"Nothing much. Obsessive, they said, so they took it away."

"What? Why?"

"Can you get me another? Got to be Rider-Waite-Smith. You know them?"

Ah. Got it. "The Tarot pack you used that day we worked together."

"Whatever."

"Okay, I'll ask the staff-"

"DON"T ask them ANYTHING. Just get it and bring it to me. Don't trust them. Go on, go and buy them. Please..." He started crying. It was unbearable.

His psych said the Tarot took him away from the reality of his daily life and that didn't help with his paranoid delusions.

"About someone called Terry."

It bloody would be, I thought bitterly.

"Well, strong negative feelings about him are not necessarily delusional. I think the cards might actually help him."

"H'mm. Well...Okay, we'll give it a try."

Bethan and Jed had moved with their baby out of London. I had yet to settle into a regular pattern of seeing her and the child. I was working very hard at working very hard. What else to do? Get drunk with friends? That hadn't worked last time with Bethan My job meant I couldn't risk being out of control in public. People who have signed the Official Secrets Act need to be nervous of becoming drunks or stoners, at least in public.

One evening my phone rang. It was Psyche and she was uncharacteristically abrupt, but still that cool, slightly distanced voice she had, except when she was really suffering.

"Why on earth didn't you tell me you and Bethan were breaking up?"

"What difference would it have made?" I had been feeling weary, a sort of listless lack of attention to what was happening round me. Even the surprise of hearing her voice didn't energise me at first.

"I would have...I don't know, supported you, and Bethan. Now Tony is off his rocker, you are the only two people I'm close to in the whole world. You have both been...so...well, you were there so often at my lowest points."

"And your greatest triumphs. Dorabella. Dido."

"Thanks. But that was art. This is life."

A long pause. We were both wondering what to say next.

"I feel so sad that the two people I love most in this world are not together, I mean – why? What happened, what..."

"Where are you phoning from, Psyche?"

"I'm in town for a few days, before I go to the States for a couple of months."

I could see a way back into my own life.

"Can we meet up? I'd find it helpful to tell you about it from my end. I think I would anyway, I – "

"You must tell me. Can I come round tomorrow? When you get back from work?"

She sat down with me. I was soon in tears. Months of work-centred emotional restraint collapsed. My drought was over. Psyche was next to me on the sofa. She put her head on my shoulder, as she had done many years before, the second time we met. Her arm went round me. I sobbed.

"I blew it. I could have raised the child as my own, plenty of people do. I blew it with Bethan and I blew it with you."

She lifted her head and turned my head so our faces were close.

"Did she want to stay with you?"

I let the question hang.

Gently, "Well, did she?"

"No. No, I don't think she did. Was I just a succession of inadequate sperm cells to her? Was I?"

"Stop it. In fact, shut the fuck up."

She wiped my wet cheeks with her fingers.

"So many hours I've spent talking to Bethan. She loved you, Gerry, heart and soul...I expect she still does. The world moved round her. That's all."

"But Jed is such a dull little twat, he – "

"Does that stuff help?"

I shook my head.

"Then don't do it, please Gerry...don't. It's bad for you."

There were tears in her eyes. I realised that she knew too well how futile such hatreds are.

I put my head in her lap. She stroked my hair.

"I lost Bethan because I couldn't reproduce and I lost you because I insisted on trying to...to..."

With that she hauled me upright and stared at me.

"Right. Now listen. You know why you lost me...except you didn't lose me. I turned you away because I was bad for you, I... loved you too much and I could see that I might ruin you."

Her tears flowed.

"So Gerry, please don't think like that. What you wanted is only natural, you must know that perfectly well." She gulped. "Blame Billy, blame me if you want, but not yourself."

"I could never blame you for anything. Ever."

We held on to each other until the gulping and crying eased.

I lay on the sofa with my head back on her lap, looking up at her.

"I worry about you, Psyche, I worry that you are lonely. Look, I'm not being nosy...well, perhaps a bit...but do you have close friends, do you...?"

She sighed. "Do I have lovers? Am I over it? No. Though I am in therapy and I think it's helping. I want to feel...clean again, Gerry. That's more important to me than being able to fuck properly."

· I rolled off the sofa, knelt in front of her and took hold of both her hands. Her gaze was unfocussed, a long time ago and a long way away.

"Hey, Dido...come back to me."

A thin smile, and she looked down at me.

"Quick check. One. You have the most beautiful voice, the most exquisite and dramatic musical sense anyone could have on this earth."

She tried to shrug it off, but I felt it was beginning to work.

"Two. You are the most beautiful creature I have ever met."

She blushed a little. Perhaps people didn't often say that to her. Prettiness is one thing, sexiness another, but such beauty can inhibit people.

"Gerry..."

"Three. When I think of what you have been through. You are the bravest person I know. When I saw Dido, I knew that your suffering had powered that performance. I felt such sorrow, that it had to be like that. The point is, you have lived through your sorrows and accepted them and that..." I started to weep again "...is why you are a great artist and my total favourite human being. You are my spirit guide, truly. Psyche, you are."

I hardly knew what I was saying. Spirit guide? But it felt true.

She got to her feet, helped me off my knees, looked at me, and sighed gently.

"Nothing anyone has said to me for years and years, if ever... means as much to me as what you have just said. I will never stop loving you...I think you feel the same about me...and that will always be so, wherever we land up."

She hugged me long and tight.

Then she stood back, and said with a little smile, "Despite that problem with the front of your jeans," to which she gave a little flick, "we have to part now. Keep in touch, please do."

"Be sure, I will."

She kissed me gently, and left.

I slept more soundly than I'd done for months.

A friend of mine in the music business said that Psyche worked harder and more intensely than anyone he knew. The recordings accumulated, the recitals and concerts around the world multiplied. We did stay in touch but it wasn't easy. Often, it was a drink or two in the bar at the Wigmore Hall, Albert Hall, Liverpool Phil, Bridgewater, before or after a show.

I remember one evening of transcendent beauty: Elizabethan and Jacobean music. She sang with others, with a band, and then she and a lutenist took us through John Dowland's melancholy world. She finished, there was a few seconds' silence, then the first almost tentative applause. We got to our feet and the shouts of delight rang out. Twenty-five singers and musicians bowed, in a long line. They were all superb, but I doubt I was the only person there who couldn't take their eyes off Psyche. She never played the diva and that evening at curtain call someone brought her a big bouquet. There was a little bit of fussing and I realised she had untied the ribbon holding it all together. The flowers fell to the floor. She insisted everyone came back on stage and she distributed the flowers to each of them, as the applause rolled on. A simple thought came to me: I was very lucky to know such an exceptional person. The face, the body, the voice. It was all Psyche. That's what she gave her audiences, because that was all she could do: be herself.

It had been over twenty years since Psyche was raped by "Uncle" Billy. I was in Cairo for a month and I was surprised to see familiar handwriting on an airmail envelope. Psyche had written me a letter about him – or about herself.

Dear Gerry,

I'm still feeling very tired and wrung out after a dream I had last night. I hope you don't mind if I describe it briefly. I think it might be important to me. It may even have some significance for you. It's not very pleasant, sorry.

"Uncle" Billy was standing in front of me. He was grinning and sweat was rolling down his face. He didn't speak, but slowly reached out both hands for me.

I had some sort of rod or poker in my hand.

As he reached me, I could smell his sweat.

I pushed the poker into his belly. It went in easily, soundlessly.

I pushed and turned it upwards inside him, pushing it firmly, slowly, right up through his chest; I felt it pierce his heart.

He just stood there looking at me. Blood started pouring out of his nose. He was still grinning lecherously. I still hated him. He wouldn't die.

I let go of the rod. I found I was holding an axe.

I raised the axe high above my head. I brought it crashing down on his skull, as hard as I could.

I hit him right in the centre of his head.

His head split into two.

Instead of blood and brains, a small, wet, bedraggled bird emerged from the cavity, looked mournfully out at me and tried to fly. It fell to the floor, flapped feebly – and dissolved into a puddle.

Billy had simply vanished and I woke up shouting.

Gerry, what do you think? Please let me know.

My Dear Psyche,

I hope you are shaking off this strange, terrible but maybe very helpful dream.

I don't know what to think. I wouldn't presume to interpret it. If Tony were able to, I expect he would give us a reading, but I'm sure you'd agree that it's better to leave him in whatever peace he can find these days.

Perhaps the important thing is less what it means, more its effect on you. My guess is that you may not know that for a fair while.

As for me, perhaps you have laid a ghost for me, so that I can stop wasting hours fantasising about ways of causing agony to the disgusting creature who did a terrible thing to you, which stood between me and our happiness. Perhaps he is now not merely dead, but vanquished, nothing but a dirty little puddle, easily avoided. Gruesome images, but still: lovely to hear from you.

Psyche had been tormented down 20 years by images and dreams of Billy. She was very rarely troubled by them again.

Chapter Twenty-One

Flight

I was watching something half-baked on the TV; I'd emptied my briefcase on to a coffee table and had worked through everything it demanded of me. I was feeling sluggish. It had been a long and tiring day at the Ministry.

The doorbell rang and when I opened the outside door, there was Psyche, looking wet through and bedraggled.

"Can I come in?"

I took her wrists, and hauled her out of the weather. I hadn't even noticed it had been raining. I shut the door and she stood there dripping.

"Right. Towel for the hair. Hang the coat there. Blanket. I'll run a bath."

"Oooh, you're so masterful," she teased. She kicked her shoes off and followed me into the bathroom.

"Towels, bath salts," I was enjoying this all a little too much. I hadn't seen her for a few months. "Shampoo, dressing gown."

She started to take off her clothes. I looked at her.

"Out!" she said. "Just because you live here, you don't get a licence..."

"Drink?"

"Glass of red, thanks."

"Meal?"

"I don't want to be a nuisance, bursting in on you..."

"Such a pain, you are. Spag bol ok? Salad?"

"We could eat out."

"I'd like to eat in with you, it'd be so..."

"Okay. Off you go."

I fussed around in the kitchen until something like a reasonable supper was ready.

Psyche emerged in my spare towelling bathrobe, hair tied back in a long ponytail. I refilled her glass, sat her down on the sofa and sat opposite her. Give her room, I thought. I needed to know why an international opera star had found herself dripping wet outside my flat. I watched her.

She held her glass in both hands and looked down into it. She said quietly, "It's so very good to see you, Gerry. I only see you three or four times a year and yet you turn out to be my pole star. And here I am."

"Yeah, well I was going to watch 'Only Fools and Horses,' so get on with it...spill the beans."

Long pause.

"I'm thinking I'll quit. Performing, I mean."

I felt panicky. "Are you unwell? Is your voice ok? Are you wanting to stop while you're at the top? Do you..." I tailed off. Listen to her, Gerry, and hold your tongue.

"I've been wondering how to tell you. I don't mind about the others, but you..."

"The others? Your entourage, your manager...or do you mean any-one who has ears?"

She smiled. "Just shut up a minute, Gerry. I've got a little speech for you."

I waited.

She spoke carefully, quite slowly, pausing to watch me take in what she was saying.

"I am at the top of my tree, as you say. And as you know, I work terribly hard, to the limits of my physique and my voice. I've had to stop and slow down a couple of times, take a rest."

She paused.

"In musical terms, I've recorded and performed most of the stuff I wanted to. I'd always like to sing more Handel and I wish someone would invite me to join a team for the St Matthew Passion, but no mind. I've enjoyed some Bach cantatas."

"So far, so brilliant."

"Yes, okay, but I think, and so does my therapist, that what I've been doing is running. Filling my life with singing, on the run, away from..."

She looked at the floor. I waited.

"From...?" I couldn't hold off any longer.

She looked almost desperate.

"Do I have to spell it out to you?"

"From...from Uncle Billy?"

"Yes, up to a point, though since that dream, and since I've under-stood that's one of my drivers, it's easier to...come to terms with it. Him."

"Well, I still want to kill him."

She looked up. "It was easy to hate him, Gerry. And in the end, easy to let go of the hatred."

She sighed.

"But?" I said.

"It's not very good for a girl to watch her father gunned down in front of her."

"Oh my poor..." I started towards her. She held up a hand.

"Particularly when, for years, I felt, not so much hatred for George, but just...I was cold towards him, quite deliberately. I made sure he felt the cold. How could he? Have done nothing? And then the trial, the humiliation...but, Gerry, I never had a chance to tell him I forgave him. Though I wasn't sure I ever did."

I felt desperate. I'd always looked up to George. He'd been a constant in my life but I hadn't really looked, I realised abruptly, I hadn't looked honestly at who he was and what he had done, and not done. I hadn't really taken in what was wrong with his relationship with his daughter. He had been the figure in my life that I needed him to be.

"Oh, Psyche. Oh, George. I'm so very sorry. It was beyond an adolescent boy, this adolescent boy anyway, to make sense of how you were with him, even after you'd...told me about it. I'm so sorry."

I thought about it for a long minute.

"So because he did nothing, was there maybe a bit of you that thought...it had been partly your fault?"

"No. Well. I don't think so, no. I just felt...polluted. Unclean. And George doing nothing somehow made that worse. Even though you loved me. But I could be cleansed by my music, I felt. I could try to be perfect in that at least, chasing perfection round the globe..."

"Well if you weren't perfect, Dido my queen, no singer was or ever could be."

For once, she brushed aside my heartfelt adoration, with a forceful little sigh. I felt hurt, and she saw it in my face.

"I'm sorry. This is new territory for me. And maybe for you."

I thought some more. The quiet deepened. Gusts of rain splattered against the window. A distant siren moved through the night to someone else's crisis. This crisis, ours, would need no blue lights. Mostly, I've never thought it true that "All You Need Is Love," but that evening, it was all we needed and we both knew we had that. I felt unexpectedly confident.

"Yes. A new outlook. It's not Psyche, my adolescent obsession. And not just my musical ideal. It's a real, complex, suffering, talented, brave woman. So brave. Now let's eat."

She didn't eat much, just enough to stop me worrying, and we didn't drink a lot more either.

At one point I said, "You know I once told you that your eyes were sometimes the windows to your soul and sometimes, I just couldn't read you?"

She smiled, and said at once, "Yes, on the way back from Tony's record shop."

"I think now I only see the clear pool of your soul, its suffering and its beauty."

After we'd washed up, "Like a middle-aged married couple," she said, she took my hand, as she had done once before, led me into the middle of the room, undid her dressing gown and pulled me to her.

"I'm not twenty-one any more, Gerry, this is not the body you once wept over, but..."

I knelt in front of her and put my face on her belly. She kissed the top of my head and lifted me up.

"Can we go to bed, please."

After a while, she let me - gently, gently - into her body. Afterwards, I lay on her breast and wept. She held me. We both slept soundly. The next morning, I rang in sick and so did she. We didn't get out of bed until mid-afternoon. At one point, she said, "Was I...you know...okay for you? This is new to me, but not to you."

I raised myself on one elbow and looked into her face. "You were not okay. You were Psyche. Beyond judgement or comparison. You were new to me, my new-found-land. I never thought this would, or could, happen."

"How many times, in 24 hours...can you, you know...do this?

"I don't know. Let's see."

Over many months, Psyche learned to let go and enjoy herself. She said to me once, "I can almost hear the icicles falling off me."

"You were never frigid. You were just - oh, I don't know..."

"Scared," she said simply.

She came by when she could. I asked about her career and she said she was working out some contractual obligations, such a dry term for so much lovely music, and then she would see about quitting. Nearing the end of these obligations, people in the business started worrying that she was ill. She had no new bookings.

By then what I loved about our times together, in and out of bed, was that it wasn't a revelation any more. It was a wonderful new norm for us. People at work noticed a change in me.

"Cat got the cream?"

"You'll never know."

"Smug bastard."

"Yes, aren't I?"

Then one time she came to see me, she looked weary, strained.

"Do you mind if we don't, tonight?"

"Psyche, of course I don't mind."

"Lovely man. Just hold me and shut up."

So I did. I couldn't ask her what was up.

The next morning, she got up, I made her some breakfast and as she left, I said "When next?"

She came and kissed me so gently.

"Don't know yet. We'll keep in touch."

"Psyche, you look...not just tired. Tense."

She put a finger on my lips.

"Don't worry, big boy of mine, I'll be okay."

She went.

In fact, she vanished. No one knew where she was. Her agent somehow found out about our relationship and came to see me. We were both puzzled. He was hurt. I felt derailed.

The intense media interest disappeared quite soon. The police said they had no reason to launch an investigation. The world of classical music brooded over what had been lost. I lived through a bleak, desolate year. Everything seemed mundane and routine. I did my work, which seemed meaningless.

Then a letter arrived. Familiar handwriting. My heart thumped.

Please don't be too troubled or hurt. You're the only one, always the only one. I just cracked up. Had to disappear. Had to be alone and unknown. Couldn't be around anyone who knew me. Not even you, my pole star. I miss you and your body so much, but I can't emerge. Not yet. Maybe not ever. I don't know. Are you crying? I am.

My Gerry. Always.

Of course I was crying. I felt sick. I tried to understand, I tried not to feel resentful. At least, all those years ago, I'd left some freesias on her pillow, not a love note that would make her feel worse.

As time went on, I was increasingly poor company. People at work, at the Club, suddenly found something important to attend to if I hove into view. I overheard them sometimes, on the stairs, in the gents.

"So bloody evil-tempered all of a sudden, can't say a word..."

"What, Gerry?"

"Yes, and I'm told his work isn't what it once was. Cabinet Office had to have a word with him."

It was true. Something had to be done.

The stamp on Psyche's letter was French. The postmark was hard to read. I couldn't make any sense of it, but I knew I could find someone to decipher it for me. It turned out to be Amiens. Now I really was a spy. How to find her in a city of over a hundred thousand? I thought long and hard. She wanted security, peace, quiet. Perhaps she still wanted to sing, or teach? She'd often said it would be nice to teach some children to sing well. I went over to Amiens once a month.

Lovely town, beautiful water gardens. I got to know the place pretty well. No sign of her. I made a fool of myself many a time, knocking on doors, phoning primary schools, even walking through the streets listening. Then, in a café over a croissant one morning, quite by chance, someone told me about the city's modern version of a beguinage.

"It's not for lay sisters or nuns, or even particularly holy women, but the flats are only let out to single women. In fact it's got a little kids' school next door. But it's still - lovely. So peaceful, you'd never guess it was...eh, M'sieu, your coffee..."

I ran down the street like an eager schoolboy. There it was, surely that was it.

A tight-faced, disapproving sort of concierge. "She does not know you are here? Madame does not allow visitors."

I looked at her and waited, until the certainty drained out of her face. "Why are you still here? She does not – "

"I shall stay here looking at you like this until you let her know Mr Haines is here for her."

"I will have you arrested and – "

"For what? For looking at you?"

Poor old thing. She was a bit threadbare. I dropped a fifty-euro note on the desk, as if by accident as I opened my wallet.

"Are you trying to bribe me?" she glowered.

"Trying? No. Not trying. I am bribing you."

She flushed up and opened her mouth but I got in first.

"It's a good deal. You can just say I forced you to let her know I am here. No blame to you."

No response.

"OK. I'm sorry I dropped that note on your desk, here... I reached for it. "I"ll take it back."

She slapped her hand down on the note and picked up a phone.

Psyche opened the door and her hands went up to her face. She stepped back.

"May I?"

She nodded, startled, maybe even a little scared.

"I don't want to intrude ..."

It felt oddly formal.

She sat down and gestured to a chair for me.

We looked at each other, and started to speak at the same time.

"I'm sorry to startle..."

"I was going to get in touch, but..."

"But?" I said.

"I wanted to wait until I felt ready and then...and then...time just went on. I got so used to my life here."

Her voice was a little hoarse.

"Your voice...are you well?"

"I'm fine. I just don't talk much."

"Yes, you sound...strange to me, as though you weren't used to talking."

She got up and made some coffee, cut some cake. These little offerings of hospitality seemed to comfort her, warm her up. She told me what had happened.

During a recording session, she got the shakes and her voice just dried up. It stopped.

"Nothing came out, Gerry."

It wouldn't work. She couldn't sing. The people round the sound desk, the musicians, everyone was concerned but she just ran past them in a panic.

"I had to get out, completely away, I daren't stop. Running again, but in a different direction. I didn't stop till I arrived here."

"Couldn't the therapist have helped?"

She shook her head. "She could help me live my life as it was. I didn't want that life any more, I realise that now."

"And that life included me."

So many times, she said, she was going to ring me. All she could manage was a letter.

"And still you found me."

"I couldn't not try. I had to know how you were and why you couldn't see me any more."

"I suppose really it is like a very long retreat. I had to have silence, solitude. I had to stop running and let my voice...catch up with me."

I felt I had blundered, was putting her recovery at risk.

"And I've crashed into your retreat. I'm sorry, Psyche."

She could hear the tension underneath my words. She smiled.

"It's so lovely to see you, Gerry. Really, it is."

"Will you come back to London? Please?"

Her eyes filled.

"I can't, Gerry, I can't. My voice is coming back and I don't want to frighten it off. My voice is me. I dare not lose it again. I think I really need to live like this."

"And I think I can't live without you, Psyche. Exist, yes. Live? Not really."

I looked at the floor. I had no idea what to do next. When I looked up, I could see she'd been staring at me. Thinking, assessing, imagining. She turned her head, looked at the window.

I felt weary, older than my years. Perhaps this was the end of it, of us. Fuck it. I can't do this any more. I stood up.

"Maybe I'd better go."

She was startled.

"Wait. Please. Give me some time to get used to...being in touch, spoken to by...the most important person in my life. It's a big thing. But maybe...yes, leave me now, for a while."

She came to me and put her hands on my shoulders. Our faces were close.

"I am so, so sorry I hurt you. I couldn't avoid it. Do you still...have any love for me?"

"Why do you think I'm here?"

"I don't have any claim, any right...you could find someone else. Perhaps you already have." She looked tense, anxious. Still fragile.

"I haven't and I won't. You and I don't deal in claims and rights."

She dropped her hands and stepped back.

"So?" I said.

"So. Come and see me again, please. In a month or so, is that okay?"

Relief flooded through me.

"That is very, very okay. Still got my phone number?"

She nodded.

"May I hold you?"

She nodded again, and muttered into my neck "Thank you for coming. It's been so good to see you."

As I walked out, I said to the concierge "I'll be back. I expect you'll get used to me."

A sharp nod. "M'sieu."

Chapter Twenty-Two

Resettlement

Over the years following my first visit to Pysche in retreat, my life settled into a pattern. Hard work, but not obsessively driven. A visit every month or two to see Bethan's children, doing the Uncle Gerry thing and seeing Bethan, who now was simply a dear old friend. All passion spent.

A visit to Amiens, where all passion was not spent but was gently and occasionally rekindled. I was hugely relieved to find that me being in her bed was not a trigger for panic, as I'd feared it might be. We were careful not to overdo it. Under her apparent strengths, she remained fragile, and I watched over her as best I could.

Back in the world of work and acquaintances, I felt a little more remote; perhaps part of me was always in Amiens. I felt less remote when some wretched journalist unearthed a lot of material about The Transition and my friendship with Tony. He more or less blackmailed me into an interview on a London radio station. He also knew about my relationship with Psyche and I didn't want him sniffing out her location. No one knew where she was, except me. A sweet secret.

"You were at least a very close friend of all the Primera family, perhaps particularly close to the daughter, now weren't you?" he said to me when we met.

"Oh well done, Sherlock," I said, "but not a tough case, was it? After all, I was in photos outside the Law Courts with her back in the 70s. Now listen. I'll give you the interview about The Transition and Tony. Not about George. And if you ask me one question about Tony's sister, I will switch off the mic, climb over your desk and stuff your feet up your arse. Are we clear on that?"

He wasn't impressed at all by the threat, of course. "I've got big feet and a reasonably small arsehole, Gerry, so pipe down." He grinned. "Next Tuesday, LBC Studios, 10:30. Keep your side of the deal, I'll keep mine." He did, and so did I. The broadcast went something like this:

'There's a revival of interest in The Transition, Gerry. Why do you think that is?"

"I really can't imagine. We're often told people need something to believe in. Personally, I wouldn't recommend anything like The Transition."

We talked generally for a few minutes and I took the opportunity to get some stuff off my chest.

"The Transition destroyed the sanity and the health of my dearest friend."

"You mean Tony Palmera."

"I do."

"Tell me about it."

So I did.

"No, it wasn't the LSD, though that didn't help. They threw him out when he was lonely and desperate. He really needed them. They treated him cruelly and, at one point, they locked him away from his medication because of some insane aspect of their ideology. It was a cult; there is much I could say about cults."

"Wasn't it merely typical of the swinging sixties?"

"I'm not sure what you mean by that tired cliché. As someone who was both there at the time and does indeed remember it..."

"Did you take acid, Gerry?"

"No, I was scared of it."

I had to bat him off like that from time to time but, in fairness, he did give me a chance to talk about Tony, to express my sadness at what had happened to him.

"Where is he now?"

"Not long ago he was released from a psychiatric hospital and he now lives in sheltered accommodation. Please leave him in... well, not peace, I'm afraid. Too late for that. Please leave him alone."

He finished off by saying that the surviving Transitionists were now running a charity that worked to clean up the environment in cities.

"Good. Pity they didn't start that in 1966 and stick to it."

"You're still bitter. Angry with them, aren't you?"

I sighed. "I just wish people understood more about cults and, generally, about closed and secretive systems of belief and action. What makes me...well, worried, more than just angry, is that this sort of thing is still going on."

"Really? Name one such cult."

"Oh no. They often have very well-paid and clever lawyers."

"There we have it, listeners. Beware of cults, says Gerry Haines, top civil servant and Transition-hater. Thank you Gerry."

The journalist did leave Tony alone but the papers didn't leave me alone. Not headline stuff but "Senior Civil Servant slams sixties mindbenders" and so on. A highly regarded weekly journal invited me to write some more about it. I wrote this sort of thing:

"I've learned a lot more about The Transition, or The Transition Sacrament, or The Church of the Sacramental Transition, as it became known, and about other cults as well. If you want to know how a cult of this sort works, it's usually fairly simple. Whatever spiritual teaching it started off with, however worthwhile its original objectives may have been, if you are looking at it in its mature state, don't spend too long on the spiritual analysis. Follow the money, follow the sex, check the power structures. Generally, they lead back to a charismatic male. He, and the group around him, expect those who join to contribute money and skills as a sign of their commitment. Eventually, the simple, even austere way of life everyone started with will become a lot more comfortable for the leader and his circle. It may become a lot more arduous for rank and file. And it's also about power over a group of people. Members will find it increasingly hard to leave, usually because of psychological pressures.

The Transition mutated, like the virus it was. It began as an apparently therapeutic activity, with a base in psychoanalytic theories. The supposedly spiritual and paranormal element grew rapidly. Some people who went through it say they were helped by it, set free from their hang-ups and anxieties. Others seem to feel it was just part of Swinging London or Chicago or New York, just a scene you tried out for a while, along with all the other try-outs available. But for the core membership, it was a lot more than another groovy scene. It seriously destabilised some people. For them, a sense of who they really were took years to emerge from the darkness and confusion in which The Transition left them. I suppose you could say that at least it didn't end with hundreds of bodies in the jungle.

After all these years, the real point is that The Transition was just one flamboyant and dangerous example of a human tendency to secrecy, unrestricted power and control. Perhaps it is Cult, as a tendency, rather than examples like The Transition, that we need to be alert to. Keep the outsiders outside, reward and control the insiders, enjoy that power. A secretive, dangerous business operation, a corrupt autocratic government - aren't they also cults of a sort?

One reader wrote in to say it was bit rich of me to go on about closed systems when I was a spy working at MI5. I was told very firmly by the Cabinet Office not to reply and in fact to "shut up about the bloody Transition, Gerry, who cares any more?"

From the time of George's murder, Tony had swung in and out of sanity. Over the decades, the sane spells got shorter and rarer, the mad times longer, calmer and quieter. After the NHS and Community Care Act of 1990, he stopped going in and out of psychiatric hospitals, but was able to survive in the sheltered accommodation paid for by Psyche and me.

"Probably better off in a loony bin, really," he said to me on one visit, looking at the floor.

"Tony, you are no threat to others or yourself, why should you be locked up?"

"Terry's furious with me. It'd be for my own protection. I'm a traitor. He's a frightening man."

"Not that frightening. He's dead, Tony, remember?"

He lifted his head up and looked through me for a few seconds.

"Hold on."

He wandered off and came back with his Tarot pack, rather grimy and dog-eared.

"Deal 'em," he said, shoving them at me across the table. "We'll see where he really is."

"But I don't...I hardly knew him, I..."

He glared at me.

"Deal the fuckers, Gerry. Friend. You remember how to."

He crumpled abruptly.

"Please, Gerry, please. I have to know..."

The pleading was more than I could stand.

"Okay, Tony, here we go."

He turned them over, nodding and mumbling. He went off to meditate, came back, looked again at the cards, disappeared again.

Eventually, after an hour of this, he sat opposite me and said "Lay down one card from the middle of the deck and don't look at it."

"Wouldn't dream of it," I said, trying to lighten things up.

"What do you mean? What - dreams? You might dream of it. You might. I DO!"

He jumped to his feet.

Always a bad sign when he raised his voice.

I waited a few seconds. He glared at me.

"Just an old-fashioned way of saying that I will certainly do as you ask. Means nothing. Please sit down."

"Oh. Okay." He sat down.

I brought matters to a head by shoving a card at him.

He laid the card face up next to the others. He stared. Minutes passed.

"Yes, he is dead. Thank you Gerry. Christ I'm tired. See you next time, man."

He took his tortured mind to bed. I drove home in tears.

I also drove home in tears from a visit to Bethan; she was very ill and the prognosis was discouraging. I had to go and break the news to Psyche.

"I must see her. Please. Tell her to come to me."

"She is too ill, Psyche. I'm so sorry."

Floods of tears.

"I must go to her."

"Are you sure? Think what that would mean."

"Take me to her."

I more or less smuggled her into the country via one of the quieter cross-channel ferry routes. She wore hoodies, dark glasses, the whole incognito star bit. But after all, she was not a pop star and it was many years since her TV heyday. We got away with it.

I drove her back to Amiens, most of the way in a deep silence.

After their reunion, Psyche and Bethan spoke often on the phone, until Bethan became too weak. The last phone conversation she had was with Psyche.

If we are lucky enough to reach a certain age, what people call a "good age," we inevitably have to go through a vale of tears. Bethan's death, our loss - it welded Psyche and me closer together.

Chapter Twenty-Three

"She's Back"

I dropped in to the sheltered housing flat where Tony lived, as I did a few times a year. He looked older - but then I expect he felt the same when he saw me. He was slightly bent, scruffy. Still the direct stare. We exchanged affectionate greetings, which didn't always happen.

"Where is she?" he asked at once. Psyche had sworn me to secrecy. She'd said it was bad for both of them when they met up. Two fragile people. She promised to come and see him but couldn't stand the idea of Tony turning up at her place.

"Damned if I know where she is," I lied, as I had done before. The Stare. He clearly didn't believe me but he gave up almost at once.

"Come in and have a coffee. Gerry, I've something important to tell you." He often did, though its significance was usually lost on me. "Something happened to me at the turn of the millennium."

Years ago, I'd have picked this up with a silly joke but it was too late in both our lives for that.

"Go on, Tony. What? Nothing nasty, I hope. After all, here you are, in your place, now." I was trying to anchor him in the present, with me, in his room.

"The 2000s and where I am...I'm spread across the years. My clock and my compass are both changed, changed utterly. Why are you smiling, you little shit?"

"You been reading them poetry books again, Tony lad? That's Yeats. Well, not the clock and the compass, but..."

"No, I haven't. If it's Yeats, it's a coincidence. Like Einstein said."

Long pause.

"He said coincidence is God's way of staying anonymous. Eh? That's good, don't you think? The Beyond must remain hidden, until it's time for me to sing it out and on. That's my part in the great pattern, Gerry."

"But that's Transition talk, from all those years ago, Tony, this stuff came from Transition, and acid, and so on. We've talked about this, haven't we, trying to let go and – "

"It's my vision, not yours." He shook his head at me.

"You won't take it from me. I need to detach from place and time, become spirit. It's starting to happen. I was Nehemiah and, once again, look. It's time for me to cleanse the temple and prepare for the return."

I tried to engage with him, see if I could lead him back to here and now. I put a hand on his arm and said, as gently as I could, "They won't return, Tony. It's over. Many of them have died, in any case."

"Died in the body, waiting in The Beyond. I know it. You could too, if only..."

And so it went on.

It wasn't that I had no sense of relating to Tony's Beyond. I have from time to time sensed something like it throughout my life. It was rather that he took a very literal view of it as a place of reunion.

That didn't work for me. It might be more comfortable if it did. "See you in the sweet by and by?" If only, Bethan. But that would put me back to square one with regards to religion. For me, freedom and contentment came from living with what is, not what I wished things could be. This understanding was a long time coming and I wasn't going to dishonour it by taking a comforting and easy road back into an organised, supernaturally-based religion. Because that's what The Transition became, ironically, about the time they threw Tony out. And if this stuff helped Tony, that was fine by me. In fact, anything was fine by me if it helped Tony in his desperation and agony. I didn't think there was much I could do to help him, but I could try.

I was told at the desk on the way out that he was less likely to become manic now. He was generally calm but he seemed to be elsewhere much of the time. He was still troubled by voices urging him on, over-riding the sensory inputs from the world around him.

Infrequently, I could connect with him over anecdotes of our school-days, or of sessions in the pub, or of the late 60s. He didn't want to return in his memory to George's flat and nor did I. That gunman blew away my friend George and after the trial, I was left with a different person to remember – a suave crook, a secretive, big-time drug dealer who didn't know how to look after his daughter.

A day or two later I caught the Eurostar and went to Amiens. The concierge always recognised me, but still gave me a stern look.

"No rock and roll, I promise."

She gave me a thin smile and waved me through.

Psyche was still beautiful to me. The waterfall of black hair was a lovely silvery grey now and it was swept back into a chignon - impossibly old-fashioned and yet it suited her well. I took her hands and we both smiled. We held each other gently, and she sighed slowly and deeply.

We sat down over some coffee.

"Thank you for coming. You've been to see him. How is he?"

I've never known quite how to answer that question about any-body, unless they were seriously ill or have just done something very unusual.

"I guess he's much the same. Moments of warmth and clarity, moments of...well..."

"Madness," she said flatly.

"He does get anxious and a bit paranoid pretty quickly. First of all, of course, he asked me where you were and as usual, I lied, and he knew I lied...and on we went."

Psyche walked over to the window and looked down into the little courtyard garden. I watched her, moved as always by her gracefulness.

"And how are you? What do you do with yourself, here all day?"

"Just the same as last time you came to me. I help out running the place a bit. I actually teach a few children to sing better. I listen to a lot of music."

She paused.

"Sometimes I croak along a bit. Sounds fucking horrible, of course."

I was amused.

"Would you sing me something fucking horrible now, please?"

"Oh, really? Look – "

"Please."

"Well, Okay, just for you. You mustn't laugh."

She went to her piano and played one chord. Then she turned her back on me, lifted and then dropped her shoulders, and sang.

A gentle, graceful, balanced sound filled the room. She finished, and turned to me.

"See? I told you I croaked along a bit. Ah, don't cry. It wasn't that shite. Was it?"

"It is a long time since I heard anything as beautiful."

She laughed. "That's only because it's me singing it, sweet man."

"Yes, but credit me with a pair of ears. What was it?"

"Handel. 'Felicissima quest'alma.' I heard Bartoli singing it on Radio 3 and I thought it might suit what's left of my voice."

We then had an argument we'd had before, more than once. I wanted her to sing in public again. She told me she'd done with audiences and pressure, it broke her up.

"Look Gerry, here's a translation of what I just sung for you: 'That soul is happiest which loves its liberty alone. There is no peace or calm for those who do not have an unattached heart.' And apart from you, that's what I think I really need – an unattached heart. Just my life here, and you."

I must have looked unconvinced.

"I promise you, I don't miss an audience. I had all that stuff. I can't go back. That's what upset me so much, when I tried again. It brought...everything...back again. All the questions, the trial, the press. During the touring years, remember I told you, I was on the run. Sing, and leave. Some people in the business were kind and you...you were my rock."

She looked out of the window again.

"And then my voice...went on strike. Not from singing too much, I don't think. Just too much...of everything. I want to spend most of my time alone and that doesn't mean I'm lonely. Well, only sometimes."

She turned back to me.

"And then you pop by, and other nice things happen."

"But there's still an awful lot of people who love your voice, your style. Occasionally, your singing is still used as a benchmark when people are writing about other singers. Only the other day, someone said on the radio that a singer "had a little of that Psyche Primera touch…"

She tried not to look pleased. I laughed.

"Oh, come on, give way a little…"

"Well, that's good. I guess. At a distance."

That was the moment the idea came to me. At a distance. No audiences, I promised her, only some musicians. To my surprise, she agreed, and worked hard to get her voice to where she wanted it.

I took her to a secluded, rural recording studio, with a small sinfonietta-sized orchestra and the musicians didn't know in advance who they were accompanying. Though when one of them heard her warming up in another room, he said "I'll be damned if that's not Psyche Primera, I'd know that sound anywhere."

I swore them to secrecy.

It was a programme of baroque and classical arias and songs. The cover was a simple black and white photo of her, looking calm and elegant. There was no big album launch, no appearance on chat shows, not even on Steve O'Leary's Radio 3 drive time slot. "He's a charming man, but it's still…not what I want."

It went rocketing up the classical charts, got played a lot on Classic FM. "It's the chill-out slot. If you've had a tough day at work and you're driving home, let this silvery voice relax you…" The BBC Music magazine simply headlined an article:

"She's Back."

And so she was.

The second album was less of a revelation, so it sold less but the critics loved it. It was, as I'd hoped, a comfort to her that so many people got so much pleasure from her singing, even after her lengthy absence from the public eye.

Two huge landmarks in her second, smaller-scale career: she did let Steve O'Leary talk to her, because she knew he would ask her about her music, not her past life and her father. She did a recital at the Wigmore Hall, which was rapturously received. A limited tour of small, high-quality venues followed. They were well spaced, with plenty of rests in between; performing took it out of her. The tickets were very expensive and every penny went to charities: child protection, musicians' charities, mental health.

I helped her to protect her privacy. I suppose I was her manager. The media badgered me but I could handle that. I was very proud of the fact that they never got nearer to Psyche than the stage door. When she was satisfied with her "temporary resurrection," as she called it, she returned to her seclusion.

And there that silver voice was silenced. She died, after a short illness and the best care I could get for her. I was with her.

Thank God she made her final two albums. I don't play them too often but before I visit her grave, I play Dido's lament.

"When I am laid in earth, may my wrongs create no trouble, no trouble in thy breast."

No wrongs, Psyche, no wrongs. You once said you were bad for me. I think you eventually knew that you blessed my life, opened it out to beauty and sadness, suffering and delight, without which no life is fully lived. My Psyche, my spirit.

Chapter Twenty-Four

Connection

I t doesn't often happen, but when it does, it's one of the things that makes life in old age worth living. I can't make it happen, I can't will it, it simply comes about. It emerges.

It's one of those days in which, as Dickens says somewhere, it's summer in the sun and winter in the shade. Early spring, chill wind, bright sun bringing an almost surreal clarity. I'm sitting on a bench in the garden nursing a cold. Maybe the infection causes slight perceptual changes, creates or adds to a certain gentle remoteness.

Tony used to talk to me about a screen between the two of us caused by my not joining The Transition. He said I was oblivious of my true self and I always would be, without making the great sacramental shift. He also spoke of the way his trance-like meditations would dissolve the screen between himself and the Beyond.

No need to ponder the nature of any such screens today. There are none between me and colours of the garden, the cascading brilliance of the birdsong, the sunshine, the light hand of the chill breeze from time to time. Eventually that state arrives which people have tried to describe for hundreds of years. I can't capture it either, but I can attempt to describe its effects on me, however clumsily.

I feel a widening spaciousness and a sense of absolutely belonging where I am, being who I am. I know not to try to hang on to it. My mind starts to figure, compare, wonder, but I let all that go, just like dropping your shoulders when they are tensed up. I can then create room for that awareness to arrive again. Which it does.

Other occasions in my life come to mind, occasions when this awareness arrived of its own accord. Sitting in a holiday cottage hearing children in the distance in a school playground, as sunlight sparkled in the water from a tap Bethan was running. Lying on George's sofa watching a pattern of sunlight on the ceiling, as in another room Psyche warmed up her voice with some gentle scales. As a child at school, sitting in a tree I had climbed, feeling safe, with nothing to do but be there. Watching waves rear up and break on the rocks of Anglesey, where Bethan's ashes went to the sea. Listening to the sounds of rain falling on leaves, roofs, through gutters, down pipes. Sitting by Psyche's grave in a light snowfall.

These past occasions seem all to be present with me at the same time on the garden bench. My life feels collected up into this one moment, this widening state of being. Nothing is sequential, not one memory then another; just one awareness. "One equal music."

A state of grace, some might call it. I don't need to name it. As it leaves me, I feel an expansive calm. The pain of years of solitary grieving modulates into something like acceptance. I know I have finished our story. I feel a calming sense of continuity, of the before me and the after me. Today's sense of meditative immanence, of the Beyond, as Tony would have called it, subsides, and will join the repeat pattern of other such times.

As I breathe out, I feel a level of acceptance and completeness that is fuller and more contented that I can possibly express.

Thanks and Acknowledgements

T he author must have some brass neck to launch a first fiction into the world at his time of life. He couldn't have done it without the invaluable support and advice of family and some very good friends. They don't wish to be named, but they know who they are. To them, all thanks; to me should be attributed any howlers and blunders.

There is some factual or at least historical basis for one element of this tale. Much fiction has been added to that basis. I am indebted to two autobiographical accounts for information about how one cult worked:

Love Sex Fear Death, by Timothy Wyllie (Feral House, 2009)

Xtul, by Sabrina Verney (Publish America, 2011)

Neither author is still with us, I'm afraid, or I would be able to thank them in person for their record of what they went through and how, eventually, they came out the other side.

I am also indebted to Neil Edwards, the director of a documentary, available on DVD, "Sympathy for the Devil? The true story of the Process Church of the Final Judgement."

Playlist

Bill Evans and Jim Hall: "Skating in Central Park," "Darn That Dream," both from "Undercurrent"

Bill Evans Trio: "Someday My Prince Will Come" from "Portrait in Jazz"

Dinah Washington:"September in the Rain" Single, 1961

The Beatles:"A Hard Day's Night" (any track, your preference)

Mozart: "Soave Sia Il Vento," from "Così fan Tutte" "Voi, che sapete," from "The Marriage of Figaro"

Oscar Peterson, "Things Ain't What They Used To Be" from "Night Train"

Rahsaan Roland Kirk: "You Did It, You Did It" and "A Sack Full of Soul" both from "We Free Kings.

John Mayall with Peter Green: "The Supernatural" from "A Hard Road" and "Greeny" from "Crusade"

Purcell: "When I Am Laid in Earth," from "Dido and Aeneas" sung by Emma Kirkby

Dowland: "Awake, Sweet Love" and "Time Stands Still" both sung by Catherine Bott

Handel: "Felicissima quest'alma," from "Apollo e Dafne," performed by Silete Venti